The Tales of Magnus and Prime

A Fantasy Novel Series

Book Two:

Meeting of the Minds
Volume 2

By Jack Robinson

magnusandprime.com

This is Paperback Edition 2021

Revised Version 1.1

Printed by Kindle Publishing 2021

Copyright © Jack Robinson 2021

Dreams and Reality: A Foreword

Dreams are strange things. Chase one too much and you'll be consumed by anticipation only to find a disappointment awaiting you, but fail to chase it enough and it'll slip from your grasp forever and become 'the one that got away'.

My dreams were like that once. I coveted something for too long and was left with nothing, meanwhile I neglected all else and found the rest of my dreams had fluttered from my grasp. It was when I made this realisation that I started to seek a new dream, one I could control in its entirety, a dream that would one day grow into the very book you're reading now.

Magnus and Prime is the proof that no matter how weird or wild a dream my seem, it can become a reality as long as you retain control over it.

Again, I'd like to thank all those that have been there for me over the years: friends, family, loved ones and now all my fans that show an interest in my work. Without you fine people I couldn't make life a dream by making my dreams a reality.

Table of Contents

Map of the Vitalands:

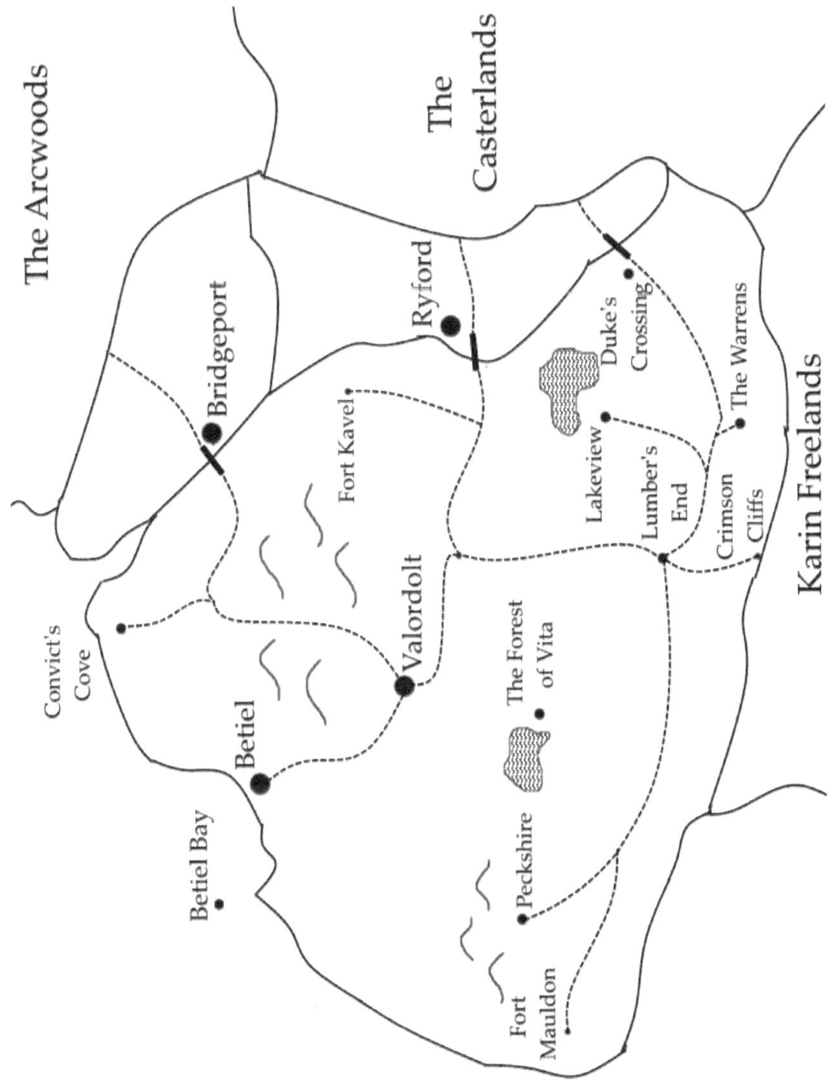

Meeting of the Minds
Vol. 2

By Jack Robinson

<u>Prologue</u>

Hericore cut through the clouds of Valordolt's skies with graceful form. His broken body of sores and boils felt a shred of relief as rain washed them clean of their poison. Life as an outlaw was strangely calming for the drake, having no limits of laws to hold him back was a feeling of equal relief.

The ground below was blanketed by the dark of night, save for distant flames of Rysin's Roost burning brightly. A haven for hunters across the Vitalands, the lodge was built into the side of a rocky cliff and rested beside one of the land's strongest waterfalls: it was pure beauty. With a windmill catching the breeze above and a waterwheel built in the fall's flow, the lodge like its hunters reaped all it could for a comfortable existence.

The Roost never slept, and its hunters guarded the walls at all times. Despite this, Hericore's approach was made without caution or fear. This trip had to be fast and he intended to kept things brief. Every minute the prisoners were without guidance was a minute he gambled the fate of the world on the backs of headless chickens. Though Helena and Travis were competent folk, anything was possible on this night of broken bonds and shattered alliances. After he perched atop the Roost's roof a flurry of voices were heard within the lodge before their leader climbed through a window and scaled to the rooftop in order to face his former Arch-Paladin.

They talked for only a few minutes, but much was said. Hericore learned of Donsis' capture and the leader's failure in returning him to the drake. He also learnt of the Warden's hunger for Kenneth, sparking further intrigue in the wayward fisherman. If Hart sought the old man, he'd have to battle the entire Guard to get him – Hericore refused to lose another man after Donsis. Lastly, the hunter asked for orders going forward as a bout of whispers bred between the two. They mentioned the destruction of Belmont and the possibility of Kalsec's return. The traveller's name stretched back to the days of Giovanni and only left sorrow in its wake.

With a long list of instruction, the leader retreated to confines of the lodge and Hericore spent a moment to breathe and gaze upon the distant city he once held so close. Knowing full well that this could be the last time he could see it, Hericore shed a tear for his home and the horrors it would suffer through in his absence. However, his heart filled with determination at the prospect of saving Magnus' future from the very curse that infested his aching heart. He had to push on without reward, for that was his true curse.

Chapter 1: Bloodletting

Hemora was the last to leave Valordolt behind due to the perplexing nature of Jelz's infatuation with him. The aggressive molluskan seemed to harbour hatred toward Hemora, far more than the average paladin. This mixed with a feeling of faint familiarity made whatever he wanted a bad omen indeed. Molluskans rarely left Tealka waters, and the ones that did made the journey for one of three reasons: a love of adventure, banishment, or governmental duty.

Jelz was part of the Order, and patrolling the streets of South Valordolt wasn't exactly adventurous, so that was ruled out. The Order loved to hire able bodies; any and all that could bend their knee to goddess or government had a place in this land. Jelz could be a renegade from Tealka, a banished man seeking glory in Hemora capture – he was, after all Tealka's veteran when it came to banished sods.

Hemora didn't have long to dwell on Jelz. The group's running pace slowed to a stop a little after a mile had passed. At that point, their distance from danger was respectable, situating them in a deep recess of greenery. Vita was a large woodland, stretching across half the Order's land.

As the name suggested, Vita was a place of life, and a dense one at that, with scores of wild wolves, hawks, bears, and fairies populating the expanse. But for every cute pup and squawking chick that lived in Vita, a rabid florankhi or parasitic ent was just waiting to overcome and eat unwitting travellers.

After hundreds of men perished in Vita, and the livelihood of the forest was tainted with half-eaten corpses, the Order stepped in. All its animals, both beastly and beautiful, were slaughtered for their pelts. Acres of ents burned for weeks, killing the fungal spores within.

Ents weren't the only plants that suffered; the paladins never took just an ounce. Glistening with greed, the semi-sentient 'God Trees' were ripped from their roots for the blessed bark they were composed of. The Order was swift and prospered greatly from the ordeal.

Harvesting the trees wasn't compulsory – they were no threat. But the Order needed regenerative wood, and God Trees had it. Although Valordolt produced the most holy, self-repairing shields on all of Magnus, it came at a near genocidal cost.

The now disgraced armour worn by the paladins was a testament to the cruel act. When the forest was massacred, the pale roses that gave their armour a heavenly white colour started to wilt. With no reliable or cheap alternative dye left, the Order now wore naked metal, coloured in jet black – a tainted shade. It remained symbolic of their declining nobility since the massacre, and nobody accepted nor denied their failure. Was it an act of the gods? Or perhaps just pure justice at its finest.

"Why are we slowing?!" Helena asked. Her words manage to wind the company of any remaining vigour, and they paused in a breathless halt.

"See for yourself," Harlan panted, throwing a thumb over his shoulder. He pointed to Rangar, who was now lying face-first on the ground. The intense battle had left the brute in bad shape, with his stomach and shoulders deeply cut, leaking a stream of blood that was running him dry at an alarming rate.

"Aww piss. We got a bleeder!" Helena said to Travis. The readjusted healer came running over in aid, his clock spattered with the Order's blood and his hands shaking in shock.

"He's lost too much. I can't help him, not like this," Travis panicked.

"That's not true: if he breathes, he can be saved. Try harder! I'm not losing another one of you assholes tonight." The girl had good intentions, hidden under her venomous guise. Rangar's body became limp and pale. The collected warrior had fought with his last morsel of strength, and now Etheriam awaited.

"See what you've done, Haruka," Lucille shouted. Her disgusted voice released a wave of heated emotion that blasted across the forest. "You wanted to kill them all, and now? Now you've been granted more than you asked for!"

Lucille and Haruka personified two opposing opinions that chose the worst time to clash. With fear in her eyes and a quiver in her hands similar to Travis, Lucille's tolerance for bloodshed was at breaking point. Their quarrel was a nice distraction from Rangar's oozing mess, but only preferable by a hair.

"Me? I got us past the Order. I saved us. You can't deny that," retorted Haruka, remaining calm.

"All of us? Ha, even if Rangar can rough it out, you took down a dozen men back there."

"Can this wait, girls?" suggested Harlan, to which both responded with a harsh, "No!"

"You think those guards were worth saving? That's bull, and you'd just be lying to yourself. *'Kill when you can kill'* is the best saying I ever learned," Haruka hissed. Lucille didn't respond for a moment, trying not to drown in her friend's macabre view.

"What in the name of all the gods up on Prime – was – that... *shit?*" she squawked. Then, grabbing Haruka by the shoulders, she gave the assassin a rapid shake. "That's not how normal people see things, you psychotic bint."

"If you think I'm 'normal', Lucille, then you've learned nothing in our months together."

"Well if you'd talked more often than not at all, then maybe I'd have realised how *murderous* you really are."

"Maybe," Haruka replied, softly.

A cross silence split the two apart. It was a lover's tiff and nothing more. Hemora had experienced hundreds of these outbursts before; they were never a permanent fixture.

Travis and Helena both continued to kneel beside Rangar's deathbed, neither able to cure their friend. But, as if summoned by pure willpower, their very own winged angel descended from the sky, breaking open the thick treeline, hoping to help the wounded warrior. Hericore looked twice as majestic and thrice as sickly in the open flats, a drake of simultaneous disease and elegance.

"Boss, it's about time," Helena moaned with a fraction of relief. "Your little stunt in the tower's caused quite the mess."

"Don't lecture me on time or the tower, Helena. I've been waiting hours for you to arrive, only to see my home be consumed by arcane fires," Hericore disciplined, with little effect.

"Philip told you the Order would call your bluff–"

"I'm aware of your partner's suggestions, Helena. But remember, Philip was also the one to recommend bombs; I wanted to lock the place with a magic seal, and I–"

The Guard squabbled for a time, and rotated the blame from Hericore to

Philip and back again. It was all rather pointless; the tower was gone now, and arguing wasn't going to bring it back.

"Sir, you must help us. Rangar has nothing left," Travis interrupted. His words were panicked but courteous, treating the drake like Bethany herself.

But Rangar refused treatment. He was a proud man, even now.

"No, I've lived far past my time. The world rejected me from birth. Now it's time to meet expectation at long last."

How anyone could accept death baffled Hemora. He'd spent so long dancing with the dark beyond that the thought of the music stopping wasn't fathomable, not anymore. The gift of life shouldn't be squandered, not for sorrow or pain – even age wasn't an excuse.

"You swore to follow my orders, Randell. I'm ordering you to live," Hericore denied. The drake then placed his claw out, above the dying body. "Do what needs to be done."

Travis opened a clerical tome and began to surrender himself to Bethany, becoming a conduit for her divine power. The life of a priest was that of submission, forever rendering to gods for the benefit of their fellow man. It was a life Travis seemed to be content with.

"One hand gives us life, the other requires it. Blessed Bethany, may you stay your hand this day! For your hearty men shall never quit!" Travis chanted, repeating it several times over, each with more rhythm.

"Death waits for those without life. Take not the folly of youth, but of the drake's blood," Hericore added, sealing the request.

A red aura surrounded all three: the doctor, the patient, and the donor. It compressed inwards at Hericore's gut, then blasted outward, pushing past Hemora and the others. The red wave had a quiet heat to it that burned at the end of Hericore's chest banner, shortening it and drawing ever closer to the symbol at its centre.

Infused with a feeling of separation, the wave then began ripping at everyone's hearts; they felt lost to the winds before slowly returning to place.

Rangar lurched forwarded, taking in a huge breath of air, akin to a baby's first gasps when it came thrashing into the world. However, babies seemed to manage it with more grace, and Rangar fell face-first to the dirt once more; alive, but humiliated as well.

"Helluva thing," Lucille gawked, along with several mirrored praises from Kenneth and Haruka.

Feeling empty inside, Hemora dropped to his hands and knees, left staring at the blood pool that surround the miraculous scene. The green grass was stained red, and from feet away he inhaled the last of the smell of the sweet ichor that dripped from Rangar's sealed wounds. The scent entered his nose and slipped into his mouth, continuously caressing his taste buds with an aromatic lustre, a lustre all too common to him.

The iron was a stern taste that complemented the sourness of the plasma, but Hemora knew he couldn't give into temptation and try some, not even a drop. This counted even more so for Rangar's blood, as his skin condition left the blood toxic, surely afflicting others with the same scaly curse.

Travis dived across the blood-soaked grass, concerned with his boss' own frailty.

"Sir, are you-"

"I'll live. Help Randell," groaned Hericore, not seeming entirely sure if the words he'd spoken were true. Whatever magic or miracle saved Rangar, it wasn't painless, nor did it look risk free. Donor and patient were both barely breathing.

Using the powers of Bethany to close the large gashes upon the torso, Travis stabilised the scaly mass of muscle, single-handedly saving him from a return to the jaws of death.

"He's gonna need more blood. My holy hands can patch him up, even send some drops back, but... banjanxed as he is, he'll need a transfusion to last the night," Travis said.

"So we need a blood sack. Any volunteers?" asked Helena.

Hemora would love to help his friend, but being of a different species limited his blood-letting capabilities. Harlan would also be excluded due to his pyrus-thick blood, which would've been close to boiling point – thicker veins evolved with addiction. Rangar was a hardy mass, but wouldn't survive being burned from the inside out once years of concentrated crystals hit his clean system.

Eventually, Kenneth came forward and accepted the honour, rolling up his leather sleeve, willing to sacrifice his strength for the greater good.

"Might as well help. Somehow," Kenneth said hesitantly.

"Let's hope your blood isn't as slow on the draw as you," Helena mocked.

"She's got a point," Harlan agreed. "If you fumble with your belt buckle in a similar fashion, that explains the stench you carry."

"It's a lot harder than it looks," frowned the aged fisherman.

Harlan smiled back. "I'm sure it is. Old age gets us all eventually, pal. I've been wearing reach-me-downs with a tight fit for centuries now."

"If we're done mocking the man who's gonna save my life, can we get this over with?" Rangar whispered from his dying state in the dirt.

"Too right. Some tubing, a manual pump and a little faith should do it," said Travis, pulling just that from his satchel; a novel bag, with a golden heart stitched to the front. The cleric hooked the two men up to a hand-pumped device and got to work pushing it in a rhythm similar to a heartbeat. "Now, we wait."

Taking a tired seat on an old log, Kenneth didn't welcome the vague nature of the transfusion.

"Till what?"

"Well, either Rangar stands up or you pass out. Let's pray it's the former."

"Heh, pray to whom: you or Blessed Bethany?" Rangar added.

Kenneth let his withered, experienced blood flow into younger veins. The whole ordeal began to unnerve Hemora more and more, and he took a walk to 'secure the area', and admittedly to separate himself from the seductive sight of blood.

***

Trees in the forest had grown rampant over the years, without animals to feed on them. Some pines stretched higher than Valordolt's walls, and all of them were thick beasts; lumberjacks would sell their heart and soul to have a chance at culling Vita. Old trials and wood bridges stretched over the flora and pitiful streams of clear water. Each step revealed a new scene to Hemora, in a difficult quest to find a place worthy enough to call his bed.

He soon found a small clearing of wild grass, surrounded by delicate birches on all sides. A dab of moonlight shone down through a thick canopy above, and set the perfect scene for his rest: cool, dim, and free of noise.

Though a chatterbox by nature, Hemora liked to retreat beyond his natural calling every once in a while. He leaned against a young birch, all while observing the area for paladins, slowly allowing exhaustion to carry him to sleep.

The forest was incredibly dull since the Order ravaged it. No life could be seen or heard anywhere in the burrows or branches. The silence was disturbing, and sleep didn't come easy.

Time passed, and finally the molluskan could hear something: the sound of galloping and neighing. A horse was close.

This could be problematic. A horse usually had an owner, and right now, an owner was bound to be bad news.

Acting out of safety rather than valour, Hemora took cover behind the baby birch and waited for the horse's cries to disappear, but they didn't. The noises became louder and louder until the horse was right in the middle of the blue-tinted clearing.

With nowhere to run, and no allies coming to help, Hemora prepared to face the threat.

"On the count of three," he whispered to himself. "One… two… three!"

He jumped out and was relieved to see nothing but a lone horse trotting across the small circle. It was uneasy and jumped at the noise he made. No owner arrived to claim the steed, so he took it upon himself to comfort the lost beauty.

"Hey there, big guy. It's okay, I'm not gonna hurt you. I'm friendly, see?" He slowly approached the shy, brown stallion, who had a large spot of white on its rear leg. The horse was calm and warmed up to him quickly. After some much needed petting, it settled down and started to rest for the night.

"Where's your owner, buddy? You've got a saddle, so you're tame. But what happened to your master?" Hemora asked, examining the large leather bag attached to the saddle.

Inside was a treasure trove of items pointing to the missing master being a knight of Rouge Taurus. The eastern land loved to emblazon their property with a crimson bull. Crimson was the colour of the combatant, and the bull depicted the head-strong soldiers of the craggy land.

The pouch held a ruby ring, an empty diary, and an apple – all red. Buried at the satchel's base were several 'wanted' posters, all names he recognised from around Refracted Light, each with big, red wax crosses marking them.

"Your old master was a seeker of thrills. Eygon, Earl of Eastershire? He was a nasty piece of work, once upon a time."

But the horse didn't listen, being too distracted by the apple. A small note was tied to the stem, and read: *For Gerald.*

"Then I guess that makes you Gerald." The horse confirmed this with a happy whinny, and nestled in close, marking Hemora as his new – hopefully longer lasting – master.

Not an experienced rider, he was sceptical of keeping Gerald at first. But the two shared a roguish life: dead to their family, forced to live life on the move, never belonging. It was nice to share his harsh life, even with a pet.

He gave Gerald the winter apple, and no time was wasted in its consumption, the horse's bulbous eyes crossing as he ate. It looked cute. Cute in an odd and rather grotesque way.

With the possible disaster averted, Hemora kept distance from the main group along with Gerald, and fell into the deep sleep he sought. A deep sleep that would return him to an even deeper sea. Home at last.

Warm dreams soon turned to nightmares, and Hemora's night was ruined by insults being shouted from waves that cascaded around him. These insults bored deep inside. *Fiend, defiler, rapist,* they called, reducing him to an empty shell. All the pain accumulated to one big stab at his heart from a figure he hated, one he assumed to be his 'beloved' father.

That burden was long gone, submerged in the briny deep. But Jelz had persisted and carried it onto land. Hemora could run forever, but could never outpace his misdeeds.

Chapter 2: A Holy Meeting

Zarpadon planted his feet firmly on Prime, home of the gods. He hadn't set foot on the majestic blue marble in over twenty years, and luckily he hadn't been spotted by his ever obedient crystivine brothers.

Though he was still welcomed by the gods, his enslaved kin didn't take kindly to renegades, and would be quick to teach him a saddening fact. No matter how cruel a god could be, crystivines would always be subservient. Zarpadon had the same ideals – for a time, but now? Now his shining eyes were open, and he saw heaven for what it really was.

Theoline's meeting would be held in the Archives, a library the size of a city, a throne of knowledge that Theoline flaunted around with unwelcome egomania. Everything that a scholar could seek was locked away in the halls of his archive – it was all a display of its owner's intellect.

Though a wise Primal, Theoline loved to let his omniscience be known to all in reach. Most of his gifts were bestowed not to help mortal lives, but to impress them. Back in Magnus' infancy, he'd often confused impression with oppression. Zarpadon, once a servant of his, had witnessed this mistake unfold.

If anyone other than Hericore had told him to reunite with his former master, Zarpadon would have turned them down. Only Hericore, a far kinder master, was worth returning to hell for.

Travelling to Theoline's domain was easier than he remembered. The distorted geography of Prime was hard to master for most and alien visitors wasted years marching around the impossible space. The trick was to focus on the destination, rather than the journey; a simple but effective rule of his crystal thumb.

***

Traversing the jagged mountains to the north of Prime, Zarpadon spotted the Archive, sitting in a valley of the bluest grass you could imagine. It was built around a mountain bigger than anything on Magnus, flanked on one side by ocean and fields of matching deep navy on the other.

The colossal lecture hall that made the archive's body stood higher than the cathedrals of Valordolt or the Gold Spire of Yellemette. Poking the clouds, it reached the heavens of heaven itself.

Bridges linked smaller buildings into the structure, some so high they cast large shadows on the forests below. Looking up, Zarpadon saw the web of viaducts, transporting entire schools from one towering library to the other. Or so it seemed. The Archive's interior was so much more.

Befitting the grand building, the roadway to its door was made of sapphire bricks that shone under the sun. Zarpadon had spent lifetimes guarding paths like that from those that sought to steal Theoline's only valid currency. Without his knowledge, the god was nothing but an elf living among the clouds.

Zarpadon soon found himself standing yards away from the giant, bronze, puzzle door that lead to the Archive. It was the entry requirement for anyone wishing to visit the vast vault of knowledge.

Dozens of ghostly spirits were camped outside the titanic entrance, yet to pass the door's tests. Zarpadon was a solid being with little room for feeling disturbed, but even this was difficult to ignore, as the desperate cries of ethereal scholars begged for help upon his approach. They were cries that he couldn't answer; not for lack of trying.

With a cool wind on the side of his sharp face and the muffled wishes of the spirits behind him, Zarpadon presented himself before the door, prostrated with arms placed forth, beckoning the door's attention.

"Manners? A nice surprise, and wayward, you are not. Proceed..." the door said, in a deep, unnatural voice.

As Zarpadon touched the bronzed door knocker, several gears could be heard turning. Each knock resonated across the field, curving up the mountains and into the warm sky. "Welcome, pilgrim, to the Archive, home to Lord Theoline. You've no doubt travelled far-"

Having heard this generic introduction a thousand times before, Zarpadon was in no mood to hear it again.

"I am Zarpadon, freed slave of this broken land. I seek audience with Theoline, and he seeks audience with me."

"-but you must jump through one last hoop," the door continued, without acknowledging his outburst. "Meet my question with an answer that satisfies, and join the ranks of the enlightened."

Theoline no doubt enjoyed watching entire academies of thinkers turn to madness when presented with an unsolvable philosophy. The crystivine was determined to starve the god of such mental nourishment.

The door paused while a question engraved itself onto its rustic surface, burnt in with arcane energy, not unlike Zarpadon's own power. The door then read out loud.

The Archive didn't have this speech many centuries ago, which automatically disqualified the blind from entering. Oh, how things had changed. As the days passed by, the gods feigned a little more kindness to their creations.

"Who are you?" Such a simple question, sure to birth a complex answer.

Zarpadon thought thoroughly, and kept reaching the same conclusion. Every road led to an unfortunate truth, his ego ached just to think of saying it aloud.

"I–am–nothing," he admitted.

If he had a generation of free time to ponder the question, he could try to argue otherwise. But as it stood, he was nothing. Hating to admit to such a claim, he cringed in shame. A sick answer, but it was true. The most disturbing thing he'd learned after falling was that it was all for nothing. He could never truly be a free being, like the men and elves. But he was no longer valued by his angelic brothers, either. He'd reached the epitome of isolation, stuck in the no-man's land of existence; the fate of all fallen angels.

"You've chosen correctly. Step inside, and find your true purpose," rewarded the door, as it swung open to reveal the interior of the Archive. A chilling breeze blew through the open door, leaving a foreboding shiver of things to come. Leaving the wandering spirits in the shadow of their goal, Zarpadon moved inside alone, as it always was for him: alone.

Those who had never been inside the Archive would be shocked to find that the interior's design was completely opposite to that of the exterior. As part of Theoline's grand design, his building was purposely deceptive from all angles, for no reason but to parade his long list of skills. Surveying, geometry, and physics were all tested and broken in the Archive's construction.

The internal look of the building was slick and rectangular, with long mazes of corridors and elevators that led to rooms miles apart. Zarpadon once made the mistake of asking Theoline how it all fit together. The answer dragged on for days on end: all of it was gibberish about dimensional collapsing, coupled with perception-warping magic. Never was a question less deserving of an answer, but the pompous god provided one anyway.

Stairways would twist and turn, up and down, with no beginning or end. Things had never been more strange than right there in the Archives. Walking the halls again gave Zarpadon a wave of twisted nostalgia for the place and its people. The monks who learned from the libraries were the most changed of all the things around him.

In the past, Theoline's disciples were clean, with lengthy beards, tied in repeated knots. This showed dedication to literature rather than outward appearance, and a measurement of their time spent in study: if one held a dozen knots, then that was a dozen books locked into their brains.

The newer generation of monks took the idea of 'learning over hygiene' to an extreme, forgoing it altogether. Presented with dirty, blood-stained robes and bald heads with burnt scalps, these souls resembled prisoners, not students.

Zarpadon worked his way up the floors to the Hall of History, hoping to peek at the past in an attempt to better understand what lay in the future. Along the way, he saw even more gruelling monks, bearing no resemblance to the scholars of old. One lecture hall consisted of mutilated men and elves; those with missing eyes, ears, and hands were included in this classroom of viscera.

"Bethany have mercy," Zarpadon prayed, offering the condolence they needed to be blessed with.

A couple of elevators later, he passed into the halls, darker than before, but still as vast. With seven floors and spanning a league, the hall's size alone was impressive. He'd always preferred this part of the Archive's many rooms. Red candles burned a flame of the same colour from the hall's many marble pillars. The floor, also marble, was once a pure white, but now held a variety of patterns.

Painted in a red that matched the candlelight, the patterns held no meaning to Zarpadon; they were most likely a code, comprising of foreign letters and numbers. It looked manic in places, and seemed to decline along with the state of the monks that painted it. Strapped for time, he marched on, passing off the illegible scrawls as just that.

All recorded events past, present, and future were recorded in this hall. Theoline knew of the Great War before its conception in Wilhelm's mind, and even held knowledge of Magnus' eventual end. If a mortal man gazed upon one book holding the future, the resulting ramifications would be catastrophic. Zarpadon, however, was never a man, and cared not for catastrophe.

It didn't take long to find the bookcase recording Magnus' current history. Insight on Giovanni or Barsalt could prove useful. The Matter Stone was a thing of rumour, after all; its place in Barsalt's hand could be a fabric or half-formed truth.

"Let's see here. The sixth era, year one-hundred and fifteen, day sixty-three," he mumbled, before being cut off by a shocking revelation. All the remaining books were missing; Magnus' future was missing.

How could so many important tomes just vanish? He even searched for any defensive, illusionary charm at work – after all, the records were sensitive. But his search was to no avail.

As he scoured the empty bookcases for clues, his actions became more erratic. His haste increased, yet speed his did not. Anger rose within his crystal insides, rare to experience, but not unwelcome. Rage was a powerful feeling, one that few crystivines could ever hope to achieve. Several hopeless sweeps later, a finger, cold as clay, tapped him on the shoulder.

Behind him was a stout, hairless woman, with a rather clean look, given what he'd already seen. Dressed in citrus-tinted wrappings, she stretched a silent smile across her face, along with a deep lump on her cranium. One eye was weak, its orbital caved. Recently poked at, she was victim to a harsh experiment.

The woman wasn't Mary, but suffered a similar muteness, and held a different expression of joy – the bubbly sort. She placed a hand on his forearm, slowly pulling him away from the halls, to a lift leading up.

"Where are you taking me?" She pointed up several times before operating the lift. "I don't need an escort. I've walked this ground longer than you could imagine," he said, grieved by the statement.

Again, the woman signed in a language of body movements that Zarpadon didn't understand, but felt a great energy from. The pair were travelling far up the shaft, heading to Theoline's personal study.

The Archives never had any windows – odd seeing as Theoline loved his work, and designing Prime was his biggest piece of art. Perhaps even the gods themselves couldn't look at the horror they've birthed? Magnus wouldn't exist without it. But was a bad existence better than no existence at all?

Theoline's study. If Magnus was a child, then this was the bedroom where it was conceived: the place where Theoline liked to sow his seed. The quarters were plain and disinfected, pristine as the day they were made. Warm orbs of light lined the walls, along with several seating areas designed for group discussion. If only talented philosophers and scientists made it to the Archives, then only the best of the best made it to this room.

The curvatures of the walls and winding of the stairs all lead to a single point at the back of the room's second level: Theoline's throne. It was a throne composed of cubic white granite, softened by velvet cushions, melding comfort and beauty into one seat. It was a throne of many meanings, aside from its literal one, and looked out over a vast blankness – a white void that took the place of a window.

It was soothing just to look upon and whispered passages in various languages: elvish, orcish, even tongues from other worlds. Prayers were mumbled to the void, but nothing ever communicated back directly. As expected, Theoline himself was perched on the throne, legs crossed, eyes closed in deep thought.

The god was taller than his omnipotent leader, Gideon, and thinner than his loving sister, Valentine – he was the runt of the holy triad. But what he lacked in physical prowess, he made up for in form and thinking with a tidy head of long, ivory hair that matched the velvet of his upholstery.

The colourless locks capped off a gently-throbbing head of veins, barely restraining the free-flowing mind; he was the ideal image of a veteran scholar. Dressed in a robe that was different from his followers, Theoline blended with his chair nicely. The only darkness on his figure were the liver spots dotted on his veiny forehead, and two deep bags below ever-closed eyes.

"Greetings, Six-Three-Six," Theoline called. "So nice of you to return home after such a long hiatus."

The wise god always spoke with a raspy, artificial voice; it was like every sentence he uttered was slightly blended around its exterior, mechanical and harsh on the ears.

The mute woman knelt before him, but Zarpadon had no need to demonstrate courtesy. He only bowed to those with power, and if it wasn't clear enough in the tales, Gideon was the one with all the power. "Defiant as ever, Six-Three-Six. Oh, how I've missed you."

Zarpadon despised that name, 'Six-Three-Six'. It was a slave name to him, and Theoline knew this. The god knew every crack and chip in Zarpadon's sturdy will, much like Philip. He could exploit every weakness, with words like spear tips against the crystivine's mental armour. "That look. I can sense its very presence. A look of hatred that doesn't needs to be seen. You hate me and you hate the gods. But most of all, you hate your own name."

"I don't hate the name, just what it stands for. It stands as a symbol of my past submission, and the fact that hundreds of others are forced into the same life," Zarpadon said, spitting an aggressive zeal, tangible to even the dullest man.

"Fine. If it'll make you more talkative, then I'll call you 'Zarpadon'. A common name for a being of the commoners," said a spiteful Theoline. "That's all you've become now: a tool for the mortals of Magnus."

Zarpadon squared his shoulders against the onslaught. "Better a tool of man than a weapon of the gods."

Theoline didn't retaliate. He simply gestured at an empty stool near his own seat of power.

"I must insist that you take a seat. I don't talk to men that aren't on my level."

"You could stand... lest you're still missing a spine to call your own."

Theoline, again, refused to humour the insults, and continued to point at the stool, his closed eyes sticking to Zarpadon. Still, neither moved; each played off the other's stubbornness.

"You say I lack lumbar support? That's still a pace beyond you. *I* still use my head." With a proud pose, Theoline doubled down on his closed stare.

Theoline was in Zarpadon's head – in everyone's heads – but that didn't mean that he had control over anyone, especially Zarpadon. The tension was slowly broken by the mute girl as she escorted the crystivine to a seat, and returned to a distance safely away from her god.

"Heads are overrated. They're a luxury I can live without," Zarpadon shrugged, surrendering to the girl's hospitality.

As proximity to Theoline increased, withered, metal breaths were heard that matched the god's grating words. Something was wrong with the lord's voice; more so than usual.

"Thank you, Cait. See, Zarpadon, even a roth-chipped brothel worker has more respect than you these days," said Theoline, sounding rather petulant and rude. "Now, let us get to business."

"Let's." Dropping down onto the repurposed footstool, a rest felt nice. Zarpadon had been a footman of Hericore for the last few weeks, and breaks had been few and far between. From west to east, then up to Prime... still, he couldn't rest for long. "Why contact Hericore? More importantly, why request me?" Zarpadon asked.

"Ah, no, that's not how I work, remember? First we must gaze upon the road that brought you here." Never was a more condescending tone used, and it contained equal measure of pettiness.

"My road? Well, I believe I took the north road out of Valordolt to the-"

"You know what road I mean, Zarpadon," leered his former master. "I've keep an eye or two on you over the years. I must say I'm quite disappointed."

"Why? Because I'm actually making a difference with the Drakeguard?" So as not to accidentally betray his cause, Zarpadon retracted his need to duel wits, lest a mistake befall him.

"Oh, we both know your little plan with Hericore far exceeds the Guard's goals. One thousand years you've spent lost in time, and not once did you stop and visit dear old me."

By Hericore's side, an unspeakable amount of deeds had been accomplished. But Theoline would remain blind to them, for now. If he ever saw what happened at Fort Palmer in its entirety, things would fall apart in the god's possessive hands.

"I don't think you know what we've been up to. You wouldn't have kept that detail to yourself if you had. That's what this is all about, isn't it? You want answers."

Zarpadon had a second idea of why his company was desired. His godly master was a sick fool, but a caring one. Losing his best servant to freethinking, the very act supported by his divine teachings, should have torn Theoline apart.

The god sneered. "You know nothing. But that is of little importance. I seek the Tempus Porta, or the 'Time Stone', as your ilk call it. It is required."

"Then seek it. You have an all powerful friend who could flick his wrist and bring it to you," Zarpadon dared.

Theoline let out a sorrowful 'humph', exhausting a stream of warm air from his nose.

"All-powerful? Friend? Both of those terms are no longer true. Gideon's no longer driving this carriage. The lordly coward's given up."

Such dire news struck Zarpadon deep down to his latticed core. Prime always had problems, but this was far worse than he could've speculated. Gideon formed the world, kept it in order and balance. If he gave up, then so would the universe.

"What do you mean? Gideon can't falter, he's an undying being of infinite strength. Faltering is very much beside his title," Zarpadon asked, desperately seeking a reprieve from the horrific news.

"His physical strength is infinite. But his mental fortitude? Well, that rotted a ways back," Theoline sighed. "There are worse fates than death, especially to a god with Gideon's responsibility." Theoline turned to the void beside them, and the unknown, made of things that shouldn't be seen.

"You haven't opened your eyes since I entered. You can't do it, can you?" Zarpadon said, addressing the problem staring him in the face: the god was looking with shut eyes.

"Of course I can open my eyes." To prove this, Theoline lifted his lids to reveal two pools of milky fluid, balled up in place of his old, navy orbs. "I just can't use them," the sad god added.

"Oh my..." Zarpadon replied, speechless at this further blood-curdling turn of events. It was now obvious why the monks looked the way they did: sacrifice in the pursuit of emulating their idol. The monks were always envious, but now it was visible, their twisted flesh now a warning to the vainer portion of humanity.

"See now why I need help? Gideon did what you and your fallen brethren attempted, and peered into the forbidden tomes within the Archives. What he saw turned him dark inside."

What Zarpadon witnessed when peering into the Archive's depths was soul splitting. It was the fuel to his fall from Prime, breaking his beliefs, but not his will.

Seeking confirmation, Zarpadon asked, "Gideon took the forbidden knowledge harder than I?"

"Of course. Who do you think would fall further when they lose grip on the world? Its very father, or a pile of shining rocks? 'Tis all my fault."

"And what of his whereabouts?"

"He sits in his golden palace, all day and all night, unclean, unsociable, and above all, fearful. He refuses to do any of his lordly duties, and made sure to punish those responsible for his state," answered Theoline, pointing to his blank eyes.

"Gideon resented you hoarding such a big secret for all these aeons. I can't blame him for that. These halls have cursed you more than once, Theoline."

"Yes. My Lord isn't a believer in: 'don't shoot the messenger'."

Seeing Theoline now made Zarpadon regret being so mired in spite. The crippled god was suffering the very fate he'd been cursed on a thousand times over. Over the years, Zarpadon had joined countless others in disowning Theoline as a cruel deity, one who should be robbed of his place in life. Now the wish came true, and he felt in some way responsible for recent events. His rising guilt was wrongly placed, yet it felt like some plot to trick him into a sympathetic sorrow.

The two conversed for what felt like an age; every second felt like Theoline was just beating around the bush, saying what he wanted and asking only for what he needed. In the end, Zarpadon was just as clueless going to Prime than he was now.

"What of the history books? What did Gideon do to them?"

"They're not there because I had them destroyed. Couldn't bear to look at those forgeries any longer," Theoline moped.

"Forgeries? It wasn't the real future?"

"There isn't a future. I know all there is to know, and all I know ends this coming midnight. After that... the world starts to die."

The situation soured further. Zarpadon knew of the secrets that birthed the universe, but didn't know the end was hours away.

There was a sobering thought to be found in the end – a shared state of being for any and all people in the world, but a saddening thought, all the same.

"This can't be the end. I can't end my life in this place."

"You won't," Theoline spluttered, his voice taking a negative dive. "It's the end of the beginning, not the beginning of the end. At midnight, mortal man will notice no difference, but the world around them will... like cracks in a pane ready to shatter."

"Sounds like a distinction with little difference," Zarpadon pessimistically countered. His old master was quick to correct.

"No! It means you and that band of brigands still have time to set things right."

"You believe we can still save everyone?"

"Not everyone. The world's undoing seems to be tied to the Primal Stones.

As they decline, logically so should the world around them. If ending the king of gold can stop the end of you and I, then everyone cannot live."

As a slave, Zarpadon was belittled for his obedience, and when free, belittlement found him a second time and branded him a traitor to the gods. It all felt like an endless wheel of torment for the angel, all until that revelation. The end was indeed near, and Theoline finally saw past petty grandeur to something more.

"I've lived a very long life, Theoline. After all I've done, this is the first time you've believed in me. Thank you," Zarpadon said, softening the harsh words of murder.

Theoline sighed. "I've always believed in you, Zarpadon. It was you who left home, not me."

"I saw the world for what it is. I needed to fix it."

"Then give me the Tempus Porta. With it, I *can* fix it. I can fix everything."

Then Zarpadon realised: some things never changed. Through the sweet-talk, the gods still sought power and control. The Time Stone wasn't a toy for Theoline to break, and Zarpadon would never allow its abuse. There wasn't any apparent evil in the god's request, but then, there never was. The best place to hide the devil's face was behind the mask of god. Cautiously, Zarpadon declined.

"I do not possess the Stone, and I can't decide its allegiance."

Understanding and accepting, Theoline looked down in shame, before perking up with a fatherly smile.

"I'd recommend haste on this mission of yours, Six-Three-Six."

His words rang sincere for once. But still, that name plagued the air...

"Don't call me–"

"If you insist on ignoring my hand of friendship, then I'll retract my manners," the god snarled. "You need me and my children. You cannot face the upcoming darkness alone. Make no mistake, the Primal Stones are not of Prime. It's us versus the universe, Six."

The night was darker than had been first perceived, but that didn't mean they had to flee into the god's embrace; there was still plenty of protection in the arms of man. "I pity crystivines," Theoline mused. "Stuck between the holiness of gods and the depravity of man. You've chosen to side with the latter. I hope your choice was wise."

"It was," Zarpadon said, standing from the stool.

"Before you return to the open ears of the red drake, you should visit Hugo, Patriarch of Mankind. He is exempt from this universe and all my knowledge. If any living creature knows of the Stone's true purpose in this endgame, he would."

The godly stranger, Hugo, was secluded, and held a reputation for fleeting social grace. Gaining audience with him would be arduous, but perhaps bountiful. Zarpadon's old master still knew some things.

"Goodbye, Theoline. Take solace in these times," he said.

"One last warning, Six," added Theoline. "Hericore isn't the leader you want him to be. He never was and he never will be."

"I know."

Cait guided him to the exit, and Zarpadon thanked her for the assistance. She gave it with such zeal, it was the least he could do. It was easy to overlook middlemen and women in these times of grandeur. All the attention was siphoned by the heroes, villains, and gods, and none ever touched the people in between; people like Cait, people like him.

Now his attention turned to Hugo. This was his next step in aiding the heroes to defeat the villains and defy the gods. It felt good to be the middleman, just this once.

Chapter 3: A Knight in Silver

Philip sat stricken with boredom as he and Thomas rode south to Karin's border. With hopes of arriving in the desert land days before Hericore, the two had no time to waste, and didn't stop riding till they reached the town of Lumber's End.

It was the last big stop before Karin. Sitting pretty south of Vita, it was once part of the expansive forest, until the Paladins ripped apart the scenery, over a lifetime ago. Thomas had lived there with Travis before Helena came along, pulling them away from the humdrum life.

Travis was a grounding rod for Thomas to draw his destructive force away from the world, a trick Philip had kept close over his years alongside the Vagabonds.

Originally, the Vagabonds were all about fun and adventure, just what he needed back in the day. But now? Now all that remained of the Vagabonds were their members: Helena, Thomas, Travis, James, and Philip himself. Finding the Time Stone had turned the average party-going youths into machines of war, pawns of Hericore and the Order. The Stone was Philip's greatest discovery, but also led to the death of fun.

He always wanted the fame and honour of serving the holy faction, but not under the circumstances that had eventually actualised this dream. He'd always seen himself as special, even before Fort Palmer, but now he had far more of a reason to claim this.

During the Vagabond's time in the past, his mind was opened by the Time Stone, letting visions of the future flood in. Ever since, his nights were ruled by what would be, what could be, and what should be.

The things he witnessed in these premonitions drove him further from the safe embrace of reality, warping his perception of what 'the future' truly meant. Friends and enemies were one in the same in these dreams, both dying and lying to him, which drove him slowly to mental ruin. Waking up every morning was a reprieve, and sleeping every night was a gamble. What would he see tonight?

The Vagabonds knew of his pain, and that numbed it slightly. But he never dared tell another soul about this – Hericore especially. The old fool was bound to misuse his gift in a vain effort to save the innocent – a noble, yet foolish reason to do so.

"So Phil, what'd you think of the new bloods?" asked Thomas.

"Pretty fond of the scaly brute and the wood elf chick; kinda sceptical of the fish though. That fish is *way* too cocky." Philip assessed the prisoners aptly, and in so doing, he proved a childhood talent that he still held today.

Skimming through a person's life in a few short minutes was a trick, to be sure. But this trick was one Philip never wanted to forfeit. Combined with his special foresight, not much slipped by the lad's keen senses.

Thomas replied with a smug grunt. "Look who's talking. Your bravado almost got 'em to gut ya."

"Tough love, Tommy, tough love."

"Don't call me Tommy."

"Sure thing, Tom."

Thomas had a knack for scaring the spine out of him, and most other people too. The brute's looks were unnerving alone, but something about the deep abyss of vocals Thomas projected made Magnus quake. Abuse tended to breed aggression, and Thomas was nothing but aggression.

"You seemed to be pretty happy with the fisherman too," Thomas mentioned.

"Who, Kenneth? Yeah, he's gonna be a nice wild card to work with. More so than the others, that is," Philip mused.

"You think he's hiding something?"

"Who isn't hiding something? The very act of hiding is second nature to us now. All in an effort to save this ungrateful planet."

Whatever Kenneth said he was, wasn't the truth. Philip could see it in the old man's eyes, that familiar stare of a person who had everything to hide. Yes, Kenneth would be interesting, but maybe in all the wrong ways.

Thomas looked at Philip with an impassive stare. "You think they're unpredictable then? More so than we?"

"Everyone can be predictable. The newbies are just gonna make me work for it. Honestly, I doubt they'll make it to Karin in one piece."

It wasn't easy to like the scrappy group of prisoners. Philip found them bold in part, but also reckless and bursting with lies. Lies were an important part of anyone, but used in the wrong manner, a lie could be dangerous. He'd spent many nights reading over the criminal records for each of the seven rogues, and each one had some strange truth embedded inside them.

Hemora was listed as a vampire; something both Philip and the molluskan failed to mention earlier. After Fort Palmer, everyone was a little sick of the winged menaces.

Haruka was arrested for attempting to whack a political figure from Yellemette. It was no wonder the pale girl wanted to join the Guard; a rematch was the noblest form of revenge.

Lastly was Kenneth, the man without a past. The interest over the fisherman came from a lack of knowledge rather than a file full of it. Whatever he'd done to the world, the world wanted to forget it.

"Eh, say whatever about the old man. I'm not impressed," yawned Thomas.

"That's cos' you can't see the bull for the horns, Tom," Philip lectured, resting his feet upon the front of the cart, whipped gently by the horse's tail.

"That's another wrong'n. Ain't it 'forest for the trees?'"

"Whatever."

***

Soon, their cart halted half a mile outside the town. That wasn't part of the plan. Broken planning was a common problem that never seemed to leave Philip side.

"Why have we stopped here? There's not a tavern in sight."

"So?" grunted Thomas.

"*So*, what are we doing?"

Thomas was a man of few words without Travis by his side, and his abbreviated answers weren't clear enough.

"Over there," Thomas instructed, pointing to a lazy hilltop not far from them. A large wall surrounded the hill's peak, a miniature replica of Valordolt's. Only a pointed obelisk peeked out from over its black-bricked protection.

With mouth agape, Philip doubted his eyes.

"Is this..?"

"This is. Royland's grave: the place where legacy comes to die."

When the Order's founder died, his remains were left in an empty mound to slowly rejoin the earth below, as he requested. This changed when the common folk found his tombstone. Loyal to their saviour, just not to his wishes, Lumber's End was built nearby to expand on Royland's plain, isolated grave.

Stonemasons built a huge memorial and the walls around it, scribes left an anthology of the hero's ventures at the base of the grave, and warriors from a land over travelled there, laying down their blades before retiring. Now over a thousand weapons pierced the dirt that Royland resided in, a steel field of unwanted honour.

Philip had never seen the memorial, neither in the past or future, and this spawned intrigue; rarely did he do something that he hadn't dreamt of weeks prior.

"Well then, this is turning into a nice little road trip. Lead the way," he said, jolly on an explorer's high.

They stepped off their cart and saddled up the twin horses that pulled it. The night air was crisp – spring was in its prime. This weather served as a reminder to Philip of what he needed to fight for in this transitional period of his life. For years now, he'd drifted from dead end to dead end, hoping to catch a ride down the path to paradise. That hope was drawing closer with each passing minute.

The hill wasn't steep or slippery, kept in perfect condition by the townsfolk, pruned and flattened for that aesthetic edge. Trust the fragrant men of the Vitalands to forge such a formal look.

"You still haven't said why we're stopping here."

"You're a smart guy. Figure it out."

Soaking in Thomas' compliment like a starved plant would slurp water, Philip examined the situation and soon realised Thomas' intentions.

"That sword on your belt. That's not yours."

"Yep," Thomas replied, patting the curved blade. "Never liked scimitars, never will."

"So you're honouring a dead friend." Philip didn't know what was stranger – that Thomas was showing some dignity to the dead, or that the bull had friends outside of the Vagabonds.

"Not a friend. It's papa's old faithful," Thomas wallowed.

"Papa? Not *your* papa?" Philip asked, being rather fond of Thomas' pa, a man he'd met only once, but in a kind way. The old minotaur opened his door to Vagabonds in the early years, and Philip never forgot his kindness.

"'Tis my papa's."

People died all day, every day. If he properly grieved for each, he'd join them soon enough. Philip had no intention of dying.

"Shame..." he briefly mourned. "*So*, what did the old guy do with this sword?"

"Not much," Thomas said with a sigh, "but that ain't the point. Point is to honour 'em. Assuming you're up for it?"

"Done deal."

They approached the granite doors that opened up to the grave's inner circle: Royland's own field of nobility. Thomas, using all his barbaric strength, pushed both doors aside, allowing a clear view of the attraction. Tourist spots rarely lived up to their reputation – like most men behind legends – but Royland's Rest was the exception to this rule.

The weapons that were planted around the giant obelisk were spread thin at the edge, but crowded closer at the centre. Some still shone bright in the night's glow, and others were rusted rods of junk, indistinguishable from common scrap metal.

The obelisk was made of a curious material, black when seen directly, but shifting to a dark purple from the corner of the eye. It was a jagged material, stronger than black-iron, though appearing more brittle. The unique structure was unguarded by physical men, at least. What holy enhancements lay on it were another mystery – tempting the gods' wrath wasn't a good idea, even to a pseudo daredevil like Philip.

"Where're you placing him?"

Thomas stopped and stared at his father's blade, cheap and thin as it was. He didn't answer, and circled around the grave. He eventually rammed it into a patch of disturbed soil – not a pretty spot, but it was what Thomas wanted.

"Rest well, papa. May you find courage in Tarus: the courage you lacked here on Magnus," said Thomas. A final farewell.

Philip remembered the day he buried his own father, though his was an actual burial rather than Thomas' symbolic one. This day felt calmer than back then, and Philip almost preferred the send-off Thomas gave than his own. Fathers were nature's guides, and his guide abandoned him long ago. He didn't need a guide any more, he held others far closer than dearest daddy.

Philip's mind turned to Helena. She was a tough nut, but anyone could be cracked open, a lesson he'd learned far too soon. If anything happened to her under Hericore's supervision, he'd make the overgrown bird pay, world-ending curse or no.

Thomas was a dull and dumb stack of meat who'd always cared about flesh over friendship. Whether it be flesh to consume at the dining table or in the bedroom, Thomas treated it as a high commodity – one he couldn't live without. A vice was a vice, and could be used against the raging bull, if need be.

The last person by his side was Travis. The cleric represented a shadow of Philip's former self: all thought and no talk. It was for this reason he kept Travis' personal growth close, to shove him away from any self-made mistakes.

The four faced danger with a collective straight face. It was them against Magnus, now and forever. As danger crept ever closer, Philip had to keep them in line. Because if they didn't, the world wouldn't live to regret it.

Philip moved and stayed by the thick doors, taking in the crisp air as he overlooked the obelisk from afar. Time had spared it – not a piece of grime or moss could be spotted on its surface. Beauty was a fleeting thing for Philip. Having not witnessed true beauty for years, a respite was found in the Rest.

But sounds were soon heard on the crisp air he breathed, the clanking of plate leggings rubbing against one another, and the crunching of grass under a heavy suit of armour. An invader was near.

"Tom, we've got company," Philip quietly said, moving closer to the hulking minotaur, who didn't hesitate to draw a claymore.

The clanking grew louder, until a silver knight hobbled into the Rest, sword drawn, already soaked in blood. The knight was in a bad way. His breastplate was crumpled and his cloak partially ripped from his back. Even the sword's hilt was crushed, with its gemstone fallen from the socket. Trouble was sure to follow.

The style of the armoured knight was reflective of a Casterland warrior, wearing fluted, silver alloy from top to toe, and draping one of the Casterland's many flags over his shoulders. Seven flags for seven nations – a rainbow of nobility. This man was from the Sud de Baie portion of the Casterland, a meadowland with several rivers cutting through its landscape; Philip was also from this area, knowing the cloak well. There was a time when he couldn't go an hour without those navy colours flying in view.

The men of Caster were proud, colourful, and lovers of art. Their towns incorporated glorious colours everywhere. This combination eventually turned you into either a philistine or a brainwashed artisan of the silver land you lived in.

Art seeped into the Casterland's military too, with combatants demonstrating fancy footwork in their curvaceous suits of silver – not the most effective force, but a fine looking force to be reckoned with.

"Be ready to fight," Philip commanded.

"Think he's done most of the work himself," Thomas said, retracting his sword.

"A question stands: what did this to him?"

"Does it matter? It'll kill him, then we'll kill it."

This didn't strike Philip as the right course of action. He dreamed not of a man in silver, but rather of a blackened suit of armour, coated with blood. Turning the knight into a distraction seemed to fit his dreams, but using innocent people as bait? That wasn't heroic in any sense. He was a hero, and heroes saved lives, not abused them.

"Play it by ear, Tom..." he whispered. "No eye contact, no awkward grunts, and I'll do the talking."

"Done deal," Thomas agreed. The two trod over to the knight with a cautious step.

Through the thick slits in the knight's visor, Philip saw a man much like himself on the inside: fair skinned with light blue eyes, though duller and smaller than his. Abundant curls of greasy, black hair hung around the knight's face, dominating his head. In contrast, the hair on his face amounted to what could be called a pencil moustache, at best. The man was tall, even while hunching over a stomach wound. He must have been truly striking when full of vitality.

"Sirs, I beg of your help," the knight said. He spoke with a smooth, high-born voice, untouched by panic, thick with a Castern accent. "Raiders ambushed me on the main road. I beseech your assistance."

"No," Thomas grunted, without emotion. It was often Philip's job to compensate for the minotaur's lack of social graces wherever strangers were involved. The raging bull was naught but a docile longhorn amongst friends, but when an unknown element wandered by, things could get heated.

"What my friend means is, not unless you can help us in return."

"Yes, yes I can. I have twenty casts right here, another forty awaiting me south. Please–they draw near," begged the knight.

"Whatever," Thomas said, retrieving his sword for a second time.

"Many thanks," cheered the knight, "and watch out for the hounds."

With a dull stab of fear, Philip repeated, "Hounds?" But his suspicions were confirmed when the yells of men and the rabid barks of dogs came over the hill. "I'm ah... not too sharp with a sword. I'll let you two handle this part," Philip said, taking a few, lengthy step backwards.

"All the reward, none of the risk?" Thomas guessed.

"You know me too well."

As was the norm, Philip backed behind his meat shield and the knight, who still wished to fight, despite his wounds.

The silver soldier had a blade that balanced on the border of what classed as a sword and what classed as a rapier, having a thin point, but a thicker base. Along with a shield twisted into obscurity like the knight's breastplate, Philip felt secure behind this professional killer.

What followed was a bloody slaughter. Thomas cleaved straight through three men in twice as many seconds, halving them into six neat piles of gore. Wearing red suited Thomas, an outfit he wore all too often. The knight duelled with a man and his dog, winning the fight with a swift chain of ripostes to counter dancing – ineffective and pretty.

The surviving raider ran for dear life down the hill, but couldn't outpace a charging minotaur. Thomas ran her down, then ran her through with his sword, ending the skirmish. With the smell of insides filling the once fresh air, Philip moved back to the cart, with the knight at his heels.

"I am indebted to you, kind sir. You and your... demonic defender, here."

Philip, the starved plant that he was, lapped up the knight's words for as long as he could, before they became irritating to hear.

"Okay, guy, I'm going to take that reward now. I'm no crook, so just give me ten casts and be on your way."

It felt like a reasonable thing to ask. With that extra silver, taking on Barsalt would be that much easier, and with Hericore's hesitation, more money could only breed fewer problems. The knight handed over the casts, smiling with a wide grin – he was grateful, but clingy, holding a gaze that wandered all the way to their cart.

"What kind of cargo are you folks shifting tonight?" the knight asked.

"We're transporting some tools and seed to the farmers down near Mauldon's Fort," Philip answered briskly, so as not to let his new guise slip.

"Just you two, or were you jumped by men of the road also?"

"Just us. Keep the numbers low and the pay high, is what I say."

The knight gave a look of concern and his gaze scanned over the meagre supplies in the back: mostly an assortment of junk James had thrown together the day before. The knight examined the junk with a vigilant eye, turning his back on the Drakeguard in the hope of uncovering their lie.

"Three small sacks of pumpkin seed, and... *ten* rusted hoes? Hardly worth the long trip, don't you think?" the knight asked politely.

"Is that a rhetorical?" Philip questioned.

"And why is your minotaur friend here armed like an Oriagus?" pressed the knight, now beginning to unravel the mediocre disguise.

"I'm the muscle," confirmed Thomas.

"The muscle? The muscle needed to protect a few bags of pumpkin seed?"

"And the hoes. Never forget the hoes."

"*Right...*" said the knight, nodding slowly. Never a simpleton, he didn't buy such a shoddy tale. "You shouldn't play dumb with me. I know exactly what you are."

"And what's that?" said Philip. He gestured at Thomas, signalling a kill order on the curious knight. A simple finger pulled across the throat was all it took to seal a man's fate, and it was all too empowering.

"You're a travelling magician," claimed the knight, turning back to face them.

"A what?" replied the dumbstruck duo. Magic was a dying art, and neither would be seen dead at a show for dullards. Why watch cheap illusions when the real thing awaited on the battlefield?

"Now, don't play silly, pal. I knew it as soon as I saw you wearing that flamboyant waistcoat. You're a wizard – not the arcane kind, but the hocus pocus kind. By dressing up your bodyguard as a farmer, you can avoid paying extra toll fees."

Worse assumptions could've been made, and Philip humoured the knight's questionable intellect.

"Yep, you've got me. Please can you let this one slide? Your silence is all we need." He'd hoped to escape this situation lightly, but it was never that easy.

"Well, the raiders chased away my horse, and I'd really appreciate a ride to wherever it is you're heading." The shining knight hopped aboard the cart without an answer. "I'll lower my pitch if you let me hitch."

"No!" Thomas said.

"Sure," Philip disregarded.

He found the task of recruiting good men was a hard one. This was why he told Hericore to search for help inside of Refracted Light. Good men had morals, resulting in complications: fortunately, bad men had none. But when Philip studied this knight, he saw potential – good waiting to break bad and be freed from codes of honour. A black knight he could be, and a knight like that would rally the Drakeguard's force even more.

"That's just swell, mon ami. I'll make good on my promise," thanked the knight.

"The name's Philip, and this isn't a definite 'yes'. I need to sleep on it," he informed, seeking insight in his 'dreams'.

"Sir Beaumont, Langdon Beaumont. Ready and willing to travel."

"Well, buckle up, Beaumont. Time's a-wasting."

"You have no idea."

Langdon awaited Thomas' return to the driver's seat. But something stirred inside the bull, feelings thought to be a foreign concept to the beast.

"What's the hold-up, Tom? I don't want more fiends to crawl upon us. Vermin love to travel these woods."

"I don't like him. Silver seems too kind for this part of the world," Thomas shared quietly.

"Tommy, there's bound to be some good men on this soil. We can't be the only ones."

"Eh, I guess."

"If you keep driving, *I'll* worry about our new friend," Philip bartered, and gifted a couple of cast to the bull, buying a lengthy silence.

The three pushed on to Lumber's End, done with raiders and done with Royland. The journey lost its boredom after Langdon arrived. The knight's loud mouth and tall tales spelled torture for Thomas, but provided a much needed distraction for Philip. Not since Palmer had he felt the Vagabonds' spirit finally return.

***

Lumber's End had old architecture dating back to the fourth era, erected from cobblestone, similar to lower Valordolt, without the tight streets and open sewage rivers. The town was one-horsed, its population in the lower hundreds, most of whom were old lumberjacks and carpenters. It once offered a great deal to the Order, but received so little in return. Housing no lords or ladies, it was the end of the Order's southern grasp and nothing more.

Lumber's End had a notable lack of lumber these days. The sign of hard work meant the end of lumber, the very namesake of this town. Without it, even loyalty with the Order wouldn't protect their land for long.

Due to the spreading notoriety of the Drakeguard, the comforting linens of an inn were a danger, and Philip settled down in the same stable he'd purchased for the horses. The floor was itchy and irritatingly flat, but far better than being discovered in their sleep by the Order.

This manner of sleeping was another gem, mined from Philip's past as a Vagabond. Being the miscreants that they were, the stable life consumed the youths. It was no surprise that he and Thomas fit in nicely, but Langdon didn't.

The knight refused to remove his plating, suspicious of a blade in the shadows, waiting to strike – a fear shared between the two. Sleeping in a casket of silver metal could never be a delight, and the stable's cold earth only solidified this fact. Tonight would be rough for Langdon, followed by a morning of aches, all for some extra safety.

Philip was like that once – the night was full of shadowy frights. But now, with foresight acting as his guiding light, he was unhindered by the ferocity of the dark.

With time to burn and tasks to finish, he penned a letter to a friend in Yellemette. Part of Hericore's plan involved acquiring accommodation in King Barsalt's land, needed in advance of their unwanted arrival. To achieve this, Philip seeded letters of deceit to several affluent denizens of Barsalt's golden capital in an effort to sway them to his cause.

Three folks were found with a profound hatred for the king they served, all seeking a strand of vengeance, and all with goals akin to his own.

"Hey, Tom, do you think I should refer to her as 'Miss' or 'Captain'? Can't decide which is less conspicuous," he asked, woefully relying on a dullard's guidance.

Predictably, Thomas shrugged, and strengthened his assumption.

"Don't ask me. I can't write... or read... or count-" listed the minotaur.

"Okay, I get it. You fail at any and all education known to man. I guess I'll just go with Captain. Best to be formal." Once settled, Philip sealed the letter, ready to pass it on to one the town's carrier pigeons. These trained birds were destined to travel miles to the golden city and beyond.

He insisted on having a double agent in Barsalt's army, a choice Hericore disagreed with. The drake wanted a more streetwise agent – one with less risk of being uncovered. No risk, no reward: the typical Hericore way.

This is why Philip wrote to one of Barsalt's captains anyway, in addition to the boss's chosen mole. Hericore was right, but Philip was never wrong, so both traitors were drafted into the Drakeguard.

"Say what you will about those flying rats, they can get the job done," Philip said, retreating to his bedroll of fur.

"Tasty, too," commented Thomas.

"You'd eat that thing? It's crawling with disease," Langdon spluttered.

"So are most whores, but I still eat them."

The knight looked vaguely sick. "Is he always this crude?"

Never fond of the minotaur's lesser traits, Philip was honest.

"All the time."

"And that doesn't bother you?" Langdon said, continuing to shun his saviours.

"Always. But I squeeze the best results from the worst people." This was said with memories of former companions lost to several more of life's lesser traits, addiction being one such thing. An old member of his company, a girl named Lillian, fell to abusing nature's finest sauce. Poppies, though beautiful, held dark secrets that fascinated the young girl. It came down to Philip and Philip alone, to break her addiction.

"Like hell ya do," Thomas doubted.

"Do you remember that night with Benny, the stable buck from Bridgeport?" Philip asked.

"Hell yeah! Me and James went out drinking with him, and the three of us woke up naked in a pigsty," cheered Thomas, displaying an odd nostalgia. "Even still to this day, I don't know where the pigs went."

"And who introduced you to Benny?"

"I don't know?"

Philip rolled his eyes. "It was me, genius. I made the best situation from the worst people imaginable."

"Eh, I guess," grumbled Thomas.

Langdon didn't seem familiar with their lifestyle. It must've seemed like an incredibly peculiar world to onlookers. Philip would have to agree with that image, as for all the time he'd spent with his friends, he'd never fit into the roguish lifestyle, for better rather than worse.

"It was pretty messy, but a fun time, though. Where did they go? The fun times, not the pigs," Philip clarified. "Seems like all we do now is kill and claw our way through life."

"Killing can be fun. Especially when your target thinks he's got the upper hand, only to land flat on my sword," Thomas said.

"Is that what awaited me when we first met?" asked Langdon.

"Yeah," chuckled Thomas. A shameless minotaur was he.

The knight blanched. "You'd really get a kick out of cutting down a clearly underpowered opponent? Where's the honour?"

"You going soft, Silver?"

"No. I just think outsmarting a person with strategy is massively more satisfying. It's better than just crushing them."

The knight made a good point. Philip had a love of breaking down a foe, all their brave threats and taunts vanishing, scattered to the winds.

"Sounds dumb," Thomas said.

"You're dumb," Philip added, siding with Langdon on this.

"Point taken."

***

The three threw more banter around for another hour, starting with the time Thomas minced a poor flute player, and ending with a tourney that Langdon cheated at, back in New Caster.

For a washed-up knight, Langdon knew a lot about politics and leadership in the Casterlands. It was more than Philip knew, but that could all be down to the five year hiatus he'd taken from home. A day never passed where he missed Sud, but when a blue moon rose, it reminded him of home.

With a gut bloated with ale, Thomas was the first to sleep. This allowed him to have a one-to-one with the Drakeguard's newest member – or soon to be member, if he had a say. As with all his hand-picked initiates, trial by insult would suffice. If one could survive a verbal battering, they were worth keeping close. If they flexed too much muscle besides the tongue, then they weren't worth squat.

"Enjoying yourself yet? The travelling life isn't for everyone," Philip said.

"Well enough. I just wish Tommy would lighten up a bit. The guy's giving off a depressive vibe, and I hate ending the day on a downer."

Philip laughed. "He's just jealous that he's surrounded by handsome faces and graces." Receiving a sceptical look from the knight, it was clear such a compliment had never met his big ears before. "I'm serious, you're a good-looking guy, Langdon. Second only to me, of course," he added.

"Heh, you have a mighty fine opinion of yourself. All that swelling can't be good for your head." Mimicking his own pause, Langdon let out a jolly giggle. "I'm serious, you've got a big brain, Philip. Second only to me, of course."

They were the redeeming words: words spoken in the wake of belittlement that always held a hint of kindness. This shiny nobleman had a fair tongue, and Philip was never happier to joust with the lance of innocent mockery.

"That's easy to say from a man laced in silver. Out of your decadent dressings, I'd wager you as a jerkin man."

Langdon nodded. "You'd be correct. Crimson, with white lace."

Red was the colour of anger, blood, hell, and all the negative parts of life. Philip, not being one to admit any love for the negative, wore a far calmer colour instead.

"The jerkin isn't exactly long for this world, pal. Best switch up soon, and save the embarrassment of being unfashionable. I know a good place to get nice waistcoats. The ladies love a dash of panache in these troubled times."

"I'll wait a little. Who knows, I might find one with a free pocket watch and inflated ego," Langdon joked.

"Over my dead body," he shot back.

"Eh, that *was* the point."

"Well then, over mine, and his..." Philip nodded at Thomas, his ward in all things physical. Langdon respected the resting bull, not wanting to mess with the horns, and backed down from the high-horse of jesting.

The knight dropped off to sleep after a couple more flagons – all while murmuring about honour and duty. A knight's code even leaked into their dreams.

Philip remained for another hour, sober as a cleric. Perception was his greatest asset, and it would be a shame to let alcohol enslave it. If it weren't for alcohol, then Philip's life would've been far better – so much so, that he wouldn't be recognisable any more. An elixir for some and a poison for all.

His dreams were never fun anymore. No carpet rides into candy land or mountains of gold – just cold, hard reality. At its core, this was what bothered him about the future: he was robbed of imagination.

Philip's current dream arrived smoother than the others, which tended to spark into his subconscious with an unsettling intensity. He sat at a table with some familiar faces: the fish Hemora, the leather-clad huntress Lucille, and a man coated in green lies.

Philip held a heart in one hand, throbbing gently, thankfully like the one within his chest. A shining gem occupied the other hand, a beauty he'd never relinquish. On the table was money, lots of it, bringing drool to his mouth. A ritual of sin and vice was happening before him, but it halted after a flash of dull grey.

The table and its occupants burst into flame as a winding snake of orange fabric wrapped around them, consuming the dream in anger and fire. Animals paraded on the periphery of the burning orange view; a goat chased several pets – again, familiar fragments of his past. The dreams were rooted in reality, but always spoke in a haze of riddles.

Like most dreams, it was cut short before the climax. This time, it was ended by one of the stable horses whinnying loudly over something in the shadows. Probably a rat or pixie – hopefully not a knife.

What Philip had seen in visions past lay heavy in his heart. Knowing what one *must* do rather than *could* do was a peculiar thing. Philip was a man doing his best, and would rise above kings and gods, if he must. Disregarding the pressure within wasn't easy, and tonight's dream didn't help in that regard.

With the fate of his future unknown, Philip wasn't worried. Death hadn't reached him, not yet. He wouldn't go down in flames. He wouldn't end up like *him*.

Chapter 4: Fanning the Flames

Ash, wise beyond his years, was left alone to lead the Gangers on a parade up north. The goal was Convicts' Cove, a sleaze-ridden town on the edge of the Vitalands. Though it was only a score of miles from Valordolt, taking the role of 'leader' made it feel twice as far.

Despite his feelings, he was never truly alone – not while he fought for the Drakeguard. James the giant and Krell the madman followed him on this treacherous path. They were not the most conventional of allies, but they held positions as two of the Guard's toughest fighters.

James was a simple man, like Thomas. Both fought for the Order, only James found little pleasure in the killing – he was far more interested in the adventures that facilitated the killing. A quiet giant, he never talked of friends and family outside of his Vagabond pals, but his stone heart never stopped aching for companionship, in Ash's opinion. He was a classic adventurer: wanting to travel, but needing to stay put. It was an unfortunate mind-set that Ash had shared for a time, forcing him to abandon all he held close.

For years, he sold the life of a family man, and in exchange, purchased the life of a soldier. Enjoying the latter too much, he soon sold out his stock of family life, and in turn forwent his soldiering career. He could fight forever, but his wife could not.

On his adventures, he refused to lead the groups he fought alongside. It didn't matter if they were Order soldiers or Drakeguard rebels – he never liked the pressures of leadership. Life and death balanced on his every decision. But now, his preference was moot, and a guiding hand was needed to keep the distraction unit moving along in one piece.

Making sure James kept his grey mitts on the time stone, Ash moved the Gangers into position for their first distraction in a little valley north-east of Valordolt. Ester Valley was a mile-long stretch of green grass slopes, and the land teemed with life during summer, with a rainbow of pansies basking under a crystal blue sky. In spring, its looks were muted, yet to be reborn; the past winter had left its mark on the valley. Still, dew-coated grass blades glimmered, earning majesty in the moon's glow.

Ester was the coronary artery of the Vitalands, connecting its head, Valordolt, to its heart and soul, Bridgeport. Carts passed through the valley by the dozen, even in the middle of the night, and it was a hot spot for raiding parties or necromancers looking for spare parts.

Tonight was a big night in the Order's calender. A monthly caravan of imported luxuries would soon wend its way along the valley's trail, presenting the perfect opportunity for the Drakeguard. Spices from the west, silk from the east, and pompous traders from Bridgeport, all in high demand, and all were targeted for destruction.

This was the story Hericore told to most, and the prisoners and even Philip's Vagabonds bought into it. However, behind closed doors, the drake told a different story to Ash and Zarpadon.

Along with all the luxuries and stacks of coin, this convoy was said to hold a much more valuable prize. One of the many travellers aboard the caravan was carrying a Primal Stone; one of mystery and legend. The fabled 'Mind Stone' had far more notoriety than the other Stones; many tales spoke of its influence and power. Wielded by an equally impressive legend, the illusive Trapmaster, retrieving it for the drake would be a mighty feat.

Existing since the first days of man on Magnus, the Trapmaster was a deceptive deviant who conned men out of their very sanity. Never staying in one place, it was fortunate that the Master would cross the Guards' path at such an opportune time.

Why Hericore wasn't truthful about the real contents of the convoy eluded him; Ash had far greater problems with attacking the caravan of traders.

It wasn't morally sound to hold up some innocent merchants, and Ash disliked the immoral. Philip wanted no survivors and Hericore agreed with this, but they held the attack in two different lights: one knowing of the Mind Stone and one oblivious to the fact.

Only it mattered little what the two thought – they weren't there, and Ash held a difference of opinion to both of them. Sometimes the grunts needed to take the lead in order to re-shape destiny. Ash was one such grunt. He turned to the troops, and uttered a new order: his order.

"Attention men–" he addressed, before remembering the Wild Cats, "and ladies. I wish to alter the terms of your service. Nothin' serious, mind, just a change of tactics." Nodding in acceptance, the Gangers crowded round. "Listen up. I want a restrained sack on this convoy. Destroy its wares, but not its people. No casualties."

To most of the Gangers, this was a difficult addendum to abide by, an unnecessary rule that bound few men. In a choir of mumbled complaints, they held disbelief under their breaths – Kat and Gaffer included.

"Ash, that's not the plan," James reminded, "Hericore's gonna be mad."

"It's not Hericore's plan anymore. I'm leading now," Ash replied, using an unintentionally condescending voice. "The caravan has to pass through the grassy hills of Ester Valley. It'll be surrounded with large trees, great for hiding and attacking from a high vantage point. I want Vipsa on one side and the Wild Cats on the other, with my men."

Praised as the best private military company out west, they were pricey, but worth every penny. One man of Vipsa was equal to ten paladins of Valordolt and everyone knew this. As long as the holy city was oblivious to their glamoured might, tonight was an assured victory, changed or not.

"How are we stopping the caravan without killing the drivers?" asked a member of Vipsa, who was glamoured as Philip. He was acting the part of Philip too well, being an egotistical brat, too concerned with proving others wrong, rather than proving his own righteousness.

"We set up a bloody faux lamb in the road. One of us will pretend to be wounded, and while the Order lends a helping hand, we'll jump 'em."

The faux lamb trick worked every time with the Order, for men bound by Bethany's religion couldn't turn down a citizen in need. Back in his patrol days, highwaymen tried this move on Ash's squad a dozen times over, and now it would come full circle, from abused to abuser of kindness.

"That's a twisted plan, but one that yields results. I can respect results," agreed Vipsa's leader. "Bol, get bloody. We need a lamb."

The Ganger disguised as Kenneth followed his boss' command and cut his palm, then rubbed the wound over his own face. Vipsa didn't mess around. Most of their guild never un-glamoured, forever a blank face marching into battle without identity or a static alliance.

"I know this alteration sounds like trouble. It *is* trouble. But the Order is nothing compared to you hardened lot. Now let's show them who's the real order in this world," Ash rallied, earning a half-hearted cheer from his new order.

He monitored the separation of the troops as the Drakeguard and Wild Cats moved to the left, hidden in the trees, while Vipsa went to the right, leaving their man Bol lying in the middle of the road. Krell became an untamed nuisance, having a moaning fit that increased the more he was around Kat.

Ash wrangled the madman and sent him to scout ahead – in search of the caravan. The gargled response from Krell was the closest the two had been to 'talking' since they met, and Ash could only hope that Krell was actually doing what was ordered.

Ash held a solid dislike for all those in the world that were too far gone, both mentally and morally. Being either made them an ever present danger to everyone, but if Hericore allowed Krell in, then Ash would also stomach the madman. With nearly everyone dispersed, Vipsa's leader stayed behind, seeking an audience with Ash to commend him for the change of plans.

The leader's name was, Opyus, and he was glamoured like Hemora, a fellow molluskan, but with a less impressive story. Opyus' name had been passed across Hericore's desk back at the beginning of the new year, an Order healer turned mercenary, from the book to the blade.

In person, Opyus was older than his records implied. Older molluskans had a distinct look to them, with shells cracking at the seams and washed of colour. Opyus had both these and a strange grouping of coral-like growths around the edges of his mouth and joints. The old molluskan's face tendrils were withered, shrunken with age, and several had lost their tip to the sword, even his wide grin was chipped away by scar tissue. Time hadn't treated him well.

What was truly telling of the old fish's character was that for a Ganger, he was rather happy in his own skin. Unlike the rest of Vipsa, he kept his un-glamoured form, marking himself as someone worth remembering.

"Boss, may I speak freely?" asked Opyus. His voice was kind and thick with a Wastern accent, a unique voice that kicked the end of each word with higher pitch and elongated the key vowels. Opyus must've come from the south.

Voice wasn't the sole thing to prove this – he wore the cotton fabrics of a southerner. A draping, cream coat and sea blue scarf stained with dark spots clothed the dapper fish. What lay beneath, Ash couldn't see – the only undergarments noticeable behind the buttoned coat was a pair of cleric's pants, an older mimicry of Travis' attire.

"You may," Ash replied.

"What you're doing, sparing the traders... 'tis a rare sight in this day and age to witness such compassion," Opyus congratulated him.

"Thank you." Ash felt rewarded for his controversial methods, a reward never given by Hericore. But, that wasn't all Opyus had to say.

"But be warned. I've seen many a good man fall to such nobility and heroism. Hmm, the only reason I'm here with you at this very minute is because my last employer followed the same path that you have started to walk."

Ash realized what this passivity meant for the mission: longer, more elaborate fights and careful ambushes. He knew the world was twisted when murder was the easiest way to deal with pests.

"I understand, Opyus. I wouldn't force this on everyone unless they were skilled enough."

"Yes, well... I'd best rally Bol and the others. Deep in my gut, I feel a horrible presence on the horizon," the molluskan replied, slapping his stomach. "Oh, and keep an eye on the Cats. Their names don't ring a bell to me, but their faces do. I don't wish to point fingers, but don't hold them too close."

"If I wasn't careful, I'd have died long ago," Ash assured him, and left for a rocky formation by the roadside.

The rain had returned, only a spittle, but enough to make the dwarf's hair dampen and flop to one side. A nostalgic feeling tingled in him, water dripping down, winds rising, and weapon in hand; the start to northern combat.

His weapon of choice was a double-sided axe, known as a cleave render, a common arm for dwarven infantry with a weighty head, carrying fine stopping power and able to puncture armoured plating. Given the Order's affinity for heavy armour, Ash cleave render would be of much use. Compared to James' glorified stone pillar, it wasn't much, but he still held it close, with pride. On missions, around towns, even when sleeping – where he stood, the axe waited in his shadow.

Along with him and James, Kat was behind the rocks, ready with a short sword and shield. A bland combination, but like Ash, she didn't leave room for form – only functionality. She and Catherine still weren't glamoured up, and with the caravan only minutes away, they were starting to tempt failure's touch.

Kat instead was busy chin-wagging with James. It was odd to see him talk so much, and tonight of all nights. Being so hulking and malformed made James quite a quiet soul, never proud to be who he was. This self-hate was evident in most giants and orcs; so a giant-orc hybrid like James was bound to hold a deep self-loathing.

"'Kay, 'kay, what about... dog?" said James.

"Easy one. Bone," replied Kat.

"Um... Arm."

"Fingers!"

"Hands."

"Thumbs."

James paused. "Thumbs are fingers, right?"

"Nope. Nice try though. Your turn."

The two babbled on and on. It was loud and a swift way to get them all spotted by the slowly approaching traders.

"What are the two of you doing?" Ash tutted.

"It's a word association game," Kat answered. "Me and the sis play it all the time. I say a word, and James needs to say something related to it, then I have to do the same with his word, and on and on and-"

Ash never saw the appeal of time-passing games like that. They distracted people from their destinations, and in this instance, being distracted from a battle wasn't the safest thing to do. A game so dull had to end, and swiftly.

"Well, would you two can it," he ordered, rising above their whispered giggles. "Last thing we'll be needing is the Order getting tipped off because the two of you keep lollygagging like children."

They didn't find his words all that impactful, and both snickered amongst themselves.

"Relax, Ash. We've got this in the bag," said James. "It's just some traders."

The urge to tell James about the Mind Stone grew, but something sinister was attached to the notion. Hericore made the knowledge secret for a reason.

So instead, Ash resorted to insults.

"Heh, sure. Just like you 'got' the situation with Haruka, then?" he replied, harsher than expected.

"Yeah, *just like Haruka*," James said, with a frown, earning him a stern look from Kat.

"Who's Haruka?"

"She's no one, really."

"You look awful sad over no one. Was she an ex-love?" Kat prompted.

"If only. Me 'n love don't mix well. No, she was some girl I tried to rescue."

James was a hard sell on the romance market. A huge slab of grey meat was undesirable enough, but with literal stone skin came its mental counterpart. The giant orc was timid, yet unfeeling when not on a mission. Kat happened by at an opportune time to see the orc smile.

"Rescue?" Kat asked.

"Mmm hmm, almost killed her," James said. "Accidentally, of course."

"Gods, that's awful unfortunate. That can't feel good." This was an understatement, and James was too lost in Kat's big eyes to see it. It was sad to see the giant so interested in a girl. Given Kat's unequal interest, it was clear she saw only a friend before her.

"It's more a feeling of... let down than upset. Know what I mean?"

Kat looked down. "Actually, I do."

With bated breath, she opened up to James, sharing a little piece of herself, surrendering a layer of mystery for the world to see. "That feeling when you unintentionally hurt someone you attempt to help. That's like a second nature to me at this point."

Her look was sadder than James'. She was genuinely grieved by something, or more likely someone. Her sadness contrasted with Opyus' own words earlier, making Ash question the integrity of the Gangers.

In a slip of admittance, Kat did the one thing a good Ganger never would: break character. "Before becoming a Ganger, I lost someone in the same way... My husband."

Ash knew what losing a spouse was like, and didn't have to speculate how bad the torture of it was, but this wasn't what caught his interest. Gaffer had told a far different story to Zarpadon when they first met: that he raised the twins from cradle to the present, never letting them leave his protection.

If Kat did marry, then she'd have to live with her betrothed – it was custom to share home and hearth. Unless Gaffer came along for the honeymoon, one of them was lying. Either Kat was telling falsity to James in order to comfort the sad orc, or even worse, Gaffer's history with the girls wasn't the tight tale he'd passed by Zarpadon.

"Gaffer never said you were married," Ash mentioned, hinting at unease.

"He didn't?" Kat said with confusion. She followed this with a more angered, "Oh! *He didn't.*"

She then moved away from the Drakeguard, back to Gaffer and Catherine, who both were sitting up in the tree line, far from the road. "I'll talk later, James. I need to have a word or two with my mentor."

"Fine," Ash called back, "but you and your sister better put on your game faces. Now!"

"See ya soon," James gleefully called, before turning to away with a grimace. "Darn. I didn't mean to make her feel uncomfortable."

James, always a martyr in conversation, was ever-ready to take any blame for all things awkward. But this time, the fault wasn't with James, and Ash made sure to clue the giant in on his suspicions.

"I wouldn't beat yourself up, mate. I think Gaffer's bunch are hiding something."

James looked dismayed at the notion. "That's absurd. What proof do ya have?"

"Inconsistency and inability. Two rather telling traits that the Wild Cats seem to have," Ash answered. "Keep the Time Stone close, I'll talk to Gaffer and-"

"CANNY CAN CAN YOUR PEEPERS, EVERYONE! SNAKE OIL'S ON THE HORIZON!" yelled Krell, as he returned from the road ahead.

"Caravan's coming," James reiterated.

"A claim founded on the screams of a masked monster," Ash doubted, never actually expecting Krell would do as commanded.

"A masked monster with consistency."

Consistency didn't mean much – Gaffer claimed to have the same, but now sorely lacked it. It was a dishonourable thing, having more faces than the split personality that was Krell.

"Right everyone, positions!" Ash bellowed to the valley.

Vipsa hid deeper in the brushes opposite, Krell joined him behind the rocks, and the caravan came over the horizon. Slowly, it passed through the valley, the merchants unaware of the ambush that awaited them.

Unfortunately for Ash and the Gangers, they weren't the only ones entering an ambush.

Chapter 5: Inferno

Kat made her way up the valley to a thin treeline, eaten away by lumberjacks from the city. If not for the greed of Valordolt, Ester Valley would be a scenic place, worthy of an artist's brush. Life was never that kind, and living west proved that true beauty was found in people, not places.

Her slip of the tongue to James, mentioning her old husband, Flan, was a stupid mistake, one that could very well ruin tonight's plans. Gaffer needed to know.

She was always screwing up, little mistakes that managed to ripple into larger waves, and it was probably the reason Catherine was the favourite. Ask Gaffer, and he'd deny it, but the evidence was there. Like Kat's own actions, it was the small things that made big waves: the way he'd speak to them, for example, and how Catherine was taught to use a crossbow, while Kat made do with a sword.

Gaffer kept her sister close – the two shared a talent for sniping. Kat and her brute strength had no place with them. She'd look over at them from time to time, and see the two talking, laughing, and enjoying themselves, all while she lay in wait of the enemy. She loved them both, and they returned this sentiment, but clearly to a lesser degree.

Flan was the only person, man or woman, to ever grant her the love she was long due. He was a gentleman until the end, but in the end, he was no gentle man. What love he gave her disappeared soon after he did, leaving Kat with the title of 'widow' before even having the title of 'adult'.

In the year since his death, Kat had found a fondness in the arms of Liquid

Courage. As the name implied, this western elixir warmed her cold heart in troubled times, not to mention Courages intended use. All recent jobs she partook in were backed by downing a bottle-full of the orange-coloured, orange-tasting vigour. She needed its courage now more than ever.

Gaffer disproved, calling it an addiction. But the old man wasn't all wise, and had never known of addiction – he had no right to call out her exploits. She'd been addicted before – to love, among other things – and knew its grip. Liquid Courage was no addiction, it was a cure.

As she approached the two other Wildcats, Catherine was mid-debate, concerned about their job.

"-worry is an understatement. Throwing ourselves against a group of the Order's size isn't a good idea. It borders on moronic."

"It may not be a good idea, but it's a well-paying one. Lords know we need it after Bjjorn failed to make good on his promise," replied Gaffer.

Kat agreed with her sister, but for an alternate reason. Catherine feared the Order, but Kat feared a more direct threat from Ash and company.

Why fear Ash? Well, the Wild Cats weren't here for a fight, and they were definitely not expert Gangers as advertised. They were in fact, scavengers. Modelling their business practice after a vulture, they'd watch as two factions battled, then slay the weakened victor to pilfer their belongings.

It was considered a cowardly trade, but Gaffer would always repeat the adage, 'If a man resorts to fighting, he is already defeated. It's our job to be the victor'. Kat didn't care for his reasoning; if it meant surviving, it was fine by her. People had died for less and won for less, too. Whatever the outcome of today, the Wildcats would stick the wounded survivors, pilfer all they could carry, and move on.

"Money's no good to us if we're dead. It'll just feed the mortician," Catherine said.

"And we'll be dead anyway without this money," replied Gaffer. The dwarf happily played with his plaited beard, and always had the habit of eating whatever crumbs were left inside. "'Sides, Kat seems to be enjoying herself. That orc, James, is keeping her happy. That's the real pay-off."

"Speak of the demon. What's going on, sis? The caravan's almost here," asked Catherine. Kat's beloved sister was a sweet person – compared to her. Having an ever-present smile, she served as a bitter-sweet reminder of Kat's former happiness.

Since her life in the west ground to a halt, she'd not yet had the motivation to smile properly, her face dragged down by too much baggage. Maybe Catherine would be doomed to repeat her sister's decisions, and Kat didn't necessarily see a problem with that. Trading a life of ignorant bliss for one of clear misery was a tough but rewarding trade in her eyes.

"Gaff, we have a problem. Ash isn't the rube you believe him to be. He's starting to peek through our ruse," she whispered.

"Darn!" Gaffer said, with restrained anger. "What happened?"

"I was talking to the giant and broke character. I slipped a mention of Flan."

"You won't even open up to us about him, but managed to go and let it out talking to a complete stranger? What's wrong with you?" Catherine questioned.

"Shut it, sis. You're no saint. I know what happened back in Telcos with that 'priest'. That slime's sales pitch was worse than anything James said – especially with the 'special' tithe he wanted in return. How anyone could call that act cleansing is beyond me."

"You promised to never to breathe a word of that. Quite honestly, I was sure you'd forgotten about that creep."

Tormenting her sibling, Kat replied, "I could never forget. I couldn't get the stains out either."

"Keep talking, and I may just let slip a tale of my own. See if James likes his flowers well plucked."

Kat scowled. "At least mine still resembles a flower, not spoiled beef."

"Girls, both of you need to shut up, right now," Gaffer said, stomping out a near inevitable argument. It always turned to spite whenever the priest was brought up. "I will talk with Ash, see if I can't subvert his suspicion. In the meantime, you girls need your glamours," continued Gaffer, "and I want you on top form tonight. No squabbling, no cussing. You're my little angels, remember?"

"Okay," said the girls, like scorned pups.

"Good, I'll be back soon. I need a sneakier peek at that blue gem James guards. I love you both, remember that," he said to them both, before leaving them to get their game faces on.

Kat reached into her pocket and pulled out an old marriage band. It was hers, made for a small, sentimental medium for her glamours. Catherine used a bracelet that Gaffer made for her – both worked the same way.

People of the western wastes always travelled, and keeping memories in one location never ended well for them. Carrying an item of pure internal emotion helped with the burdens of the past, and became synonymous with its owner. Unless the object was magical already, it made an easy glamour.

"I always hate this part," complained Catherine, as the two began to enchant their objects.

Gaffer taught them glamour magic alongside grifting, two skills that paved the way for their lives, but neither left any room for error. Messing up a glamour's chant had far reaching consequences, with some legendary failures getting stuck between their regular appearance and that of another, making for an abomination with mismatched limbs and features.

"Relax, this is the easy part," she assured her sister.

"Easy – minus the mutating effects of failure."

Fearfully, Kat reminded her, "No reward is without risk."

After chanting echoing words onto the wedding band, all Kat did was slide it on a finger; from there, a shroud of pink mist surrounded her, and the woman that stepped out wasn't Kat... at least in appearance. Her new face was dark of skin and black of hair, having the wide curves of a teapot and a slim pair of limbs. James mentioned this person – a woman called Helena, an old friend of his.

The first thing she did was measure up her new body: its height, weight, and overall shape. She didn't know this Helena, but was pleased with her appearance – slick and sassy. Catherine was stuck with a girl called Haruka, a Shen-Sumay lady with a near malnourished look to her.

"Kat – you're... *different*," Catherine falsely gasped.

"Thanks for noticing. I did something new with my hair." The two laughed at the old, but still funny joke they shared. It became a custom with every new face they accepted as their own. "And your change looks ever the beaut. The beanpole look suits you," she said, throwing herself over Catherine's shoulder.

"Jeez, sis. What did this poor Haruka girl do to deserve such a knock?"

"It was only a joke," she defended. "Besides, what's she ever done to deserve my kind words?"

"Unbelievable," Catherine sighed.

Before Kat delved deeper into a hole of her own making, the Order's carts spotted Bol, lying face down in the road.

"Places, everyone!" Ash called out.

"Shit. Good luck, *Haruka*," Kat said with a wink.

"Sure thing, *Helena*."

She returned to her place behind the rocks, mere feet from the road, while Gaffer took his place back with Catherine. Kat remained isolated from her Cats, surrounded by those that guarded the drake, and with Helena's face, she fitted in nicely.

The minute before the fight was silent and peacefully unnerving. Not a drop of sweat dared to drip from anyone's faces as the caravan rode into the valley. Still, Kat pulled out her Courage, taking one last swig before the action kicked off.

Bol was Kenneth's doppelgänger, and served as the bait for Ash's trap. Faux lambs were easy to recognise under an experienced eye, and she hoped the Order's men weren't so discerning.

But the caravan of horses and carts didn't stop at Bol, halting far from the 'wounded' man. Only one horseback rider travelled towards him, riding in from the wrong direction. Galloping from Valordolt's side of the valley, the rider didn't break pace, continuing all the way to the deathly still Bol.

"This isn't the plan," Kat whispered to Ash.

"Do you think I don't know that? Let's just see how this plays out. We can improvise."

The rider jumped off his mount standing at a respectful seven-feet tall and wearing a suit of custom armour. Black as coal, and dense as platinum, it was no traditional outfit for the Order. Kat recognised the bastard sword and heater shield attached to his back, but she just couldn't remember where.

"No, gods. Please not him," stammered Ash, knowing the black knight in an instant. His demeanour changed from focused to panicked, his dwarven lips bit together, and his hands shook.

The rider stopped in front of Bol, his pointed boots gently poking the Ganger's face. In a booming, low-brow voice, the knight spoke.

"Very convincing. *Only...*" He drew his bastard, thrust down, and impaled Bol in the process. "Your breaths. They were too deep." As Bol coughed up his last, the knight was happy. "On the bright side, you won't make that mistake again."

At the sight of their friend's death, the members of Vipsa moved out of hiding, attacking the rider without permission. They threw all they had – arrows, bolts, bullets – but it wasn't enough. The mad dog was agile, too defensive for such a huge person, and effortlessly held off the barrage of ranged attacks.

When the knight turned away, back at the caravan, his cloak could be seen, clear as day. It was that of Ryon Wellington.

"We've got to run. Now!" shouted Ash. But no one listened.

Krell and James were now up close to the Battlemaster, and began to push him back down the road – into another trap. When the two renowned fighters were separated from the rest, Wellington signalled his troops, and a dozen men charged over each side of the valley. From behind both the Cats and Vipsa came six swordsmen and six pikemen, clad in black plate.

Backing them up were a squad of rangers and clerics, spewing prayers and crossbow bolts like a dragon spat flame, covering the valley in wisps of gold along with streaks of red, as several Vipsa fighters took a hit.

"Fall back! We've been compromised; someone ratted us out! Fall back, you morons!" Ash called, but again, his call fell on deaf ears.

"They're not going to listen," Kat belittled.

"I... I know," he accepted, and charged forward. The dwarf's height came in handy as he ducked beneath several swings of a sword only to cleave down a paladin in one fell swoop. He had the skill of man who'd been fighting alongside the Order for years, knowing every paladin's move several steps in advance.

Kat dived into a skirmish with several crusaders, their breaths reeking of liquor and a look of ill intent on their faces. Perhaps their intentions were sexual – they sure seemed lustful. Or maybe, the pair sought the pride of protecting Valordolt: two noble men among the chaos.

Nobles or deviants, it was bloody, and one of them might have emptied their bowels before said bowels were severed from their body. The smell of shit may have lingered on Kat sword, but she survived. This kind of thing kept her going – the adrenaline and the fear of death that spawned it both reminded Kat what life meant. Only by feeling the end could she appreciate her beginning.

The next iron-clad moron was hard to hit, with all of her blows smacking a golden force before bouncing off their armour. The paladin enjoyed watching her struggle to harm him. He chuckled and promised her a 'quick end' before her fellow Cats pounced in to assist her. With some well-aimed shots, four clerics were taken out in just as many seconds, enabling her to finally end the crusader. Bowing to her sister in gratitude, Kat moved in close to Wellington, at the centre of the valley.

James was struggling to fend of Wellington's erratic combat style, but his struggle wasn't the greatest around – for to Kat's right, Ash and Vipsa were now surrounded on all sides, hopelessly outmanoeuvred. The dwarf had thrown his passive outlook off the wagon, and tried to get close to her, but before he could, the Vipsa members posing as Travis and Lucille fell on the tips of two black-iron spears.

"Fuck me!" Kat blurted out, in a mix of shock and excitement. Her high-pitched cry caught Wellington's gaze.

"With pleasure," the Battlemaster answered.

"Don't you dare, Ryon," James roared, treading onto thin ice. "She's not one of your ignorant whores!" The giant grappled Wellington, wrestling him across the valley and tearing up the greenery. Kat was left alone again.

Being alone in the battle was a precarious position, the purest form of isolation, able to turn a trusting soldier into a lone wolf unit in a matter of seconds, shrugging off all future help with an ever-growing addition to 'making it alone'.

With another three clerics down, Gaffer moved downhill in an attempt to reunite the Cats. His skill with a halberd was no match for his archery talents, but with his last arrows buried in a paladin's back, it was time to use his weaker talents.

"Katherine! Get your hide over 'ere, *tout suite!*" he ordered.

Kat wanted none of it – she was adopting this 'lone wolf' mentality. For every life she ended, her confidence in herself, and herself alone, grew. By the time Gaffer fought to reach her, she was dancing down the cobble road, cutting and slicing anything in her way. Her actions mimicked that of Krell, who found pleasure in ripping out a man's spine, and using it to strangle another.

"I HAVE THE POWER! The power to *rend,*" Krell yelled over and over, as he choked the life out of the rough paladin.

His style was grim, but Kat found it satisfying to watch. She moved to a young woman who barely fit her plating, and grabbed her. With the girl in her grip, Kat's mind raced with possibilities: decapitation, disembowelment, blinding, choking, limb barring... the list went on. In the end, she allowed Krell to decide.

"Hey, big guy, got a present for ya," she yelled, presenting the woman to him. It took him a second to react, but he soon jumped at her gift with a crazed stare and accompanying mouth of drool. Getting down on all fours, Krell charged at the paladin like a bull.

"SCREAM LIKE THE WEAK BABE YOU ARE! FEEL THE PAIN OF A THOUSAND BROKEN HEARTS, JUST LIKE I DID!" he screamed, ripping the girl from Kat's grip and systematically breaking her into an elven mulch pile.

"Kat, what the hell are you doing?!" Gaffer said, catching up with her at last, his breath short and his fatigue apparent.

"Having fun!" she answered, finally finding the power to smile.

Gaffer stared at her. "Fun? That was barbaric!"

"And what, picking these bodies clean after the fact isn't?"

"We work after the suffering. We don't cause it," he lectured. After one of Gaffer's lessons, she'd learned them all, yet he'd still yap on. "I didn't raise you like this... like a bandit!"

Jealousy arose where her fear failed.

"I bet if this was Catherine, she'd have a slapped wrist, then that'd be that."

"Oh, you have a lot to learn, child," Gaffer said with disgust.

As the Order's force cracked under the might of the Gangers, when victory became a possibility, Wellington dashed down their pride.

"Riders! Attack!" he called, spicing up the battle with a charge of men on horseback galloping over the hills. They weaved around the area, mowing down one of Vipsa's last members and ripping Ash's left shoulder in two. Their polished armour was reflective in the moonlight, and Kat could see her blood-coated image in the chest piece of an attacking rider.

Her blood, Krell's blood, and the young girl's blood covered her. Each was indistinguishable from the other. Beneath that was a face belonging to another woman – a face she didn't recognise, a face with a smile. Catherine shot down the rider and broke the image, a reprieve for Kat, as she was starting to like what she saw.

Over yonder, James was locked in an unwinnable, inescapable battle with Wellington. With the giant separated from his weapon, defeat wasn't an 'if', it was 'when'. He fought well, but a group of archers positioned themselves nearby and slowly brought down the pillar of stone, leaving Wellington in open season.

"You'll regret that, prick," Kat whispered, moving towards him and leaving Krell behind to 'play' with the fallen rider.

"Stay back from the big man. He's dangerous," Gaffer warned. "What the hell are you doing, Kat!"

Kat smiled wanly. "Winning."

Wellington turned his beastly aggression from James to her. His breath had the liquor smell too, but mixed with the stink of a whore; he wasn't just a violent drunk, but a violent, womanising drunk. The others had a small spark of nobility, but not him.

This was more than enough to make Kat furious. Wellington and her late Flan were both were men who lived for the bottle, the sword, and the fuck, but only one had died by them.

"Well, look at you, Miss Starr. Finally ditched that corny mask and those peashooters, 'ave you?" asked Wellington, still unwise to her glamoured deception.

"You'll pay for the lives you've ruined, you bastard!" Kat snarled.

"Will I? Does that include that uptight boyfriend of yours?" he replied, pointing to a dead Vipsa man wearing a smug grin and a head of waving curls.

"Who?"

"Ha, you cold bitch. I always figured you wanted him for the coin," Wellington said, finally readying his own sword. "Let's add you both to Tarus' pits then."

His blows were stronger than Kat could ever expect. They knocked her around, nearly ending her life if it weren't for her equal strong resolve.

"I'll admit, I'm impressed, Helena. Half my size, half my weapon, and you're still breathing. Half the men in Midgartt can't claim the same."

But soon she tired, and could hold her own no more. The lone wolf mentality only carried her so far, and an uppercut from the bastard's pommel was too much. When her guard broke, along with several teeth, Wellington dashed in for the kill. With the blessing of a god on his side, his blade would've jammed itself deep inside her chest – if not for a little hindrance named Gaffer.

The dwarf came between them, taking the Battlemaster on with his halberd, hitting Wellington with more rage than Kat could muster.

"Never, *ever*, hurt the people I love!" Gaffer yelled at the black knight, but to no avail. Wellington just grinned, blocking every strike.

"Say there, dwarf, I'm a little *short* on the old time. So let's get this over with."

"I'm not going down easy," Gaffer responded, boiling over in a red-faced onslaught. He might have won; his love pushed him toward a swift victory, but his fortunes changed course and decided to turn him over to defeat.

"Sis, a little help!" Catherine called. Out of bolts, she was left defenceless and under attack from one final pikeman.

In the moment, Kat didn't think much of it. She stayed rooted in her blood-letting madness, and this meant Gaffer had to step in. Kicking back Wellington, Gaffer launched his halberd at the paladins closing in on Catherine. Smacking the pikeman square in the neck, he'd saved a life at the cost of his own; caring came at the ultimate cost for him.

In one motion, Wellington broke Gaffer's shoulder with his heater, then used it to bash the dwarf's aged face so hard he spun twice on the spot. A stab in the back sealed his fate, and Gaffer's life was over.

"Gaff?" Kat gasped.

"No!" yelped Catherine, dropping to her knees.

Speaking through a mouthful of blood and sorrow, Gaffer gave one last scrap of advice: "Run."

Before he closed his eyes one final time, he watched over Kat, his stare saying more than any last words could. It held a mixture of heartache combined with the classic 'I told you so' feeling.

Kat screamed at the sky, ready to avenge her mentor and disregard his advice one final time. Catherine, on the other hand, was too torn up over Gaffer's passing to spread more death, and stared at his lifeless body, hopelessly waiting for him to move again.

Wellington saw Kat's anger and seemed to thrive off her pain. He was eager to take her life too. However, was denied by Krell, who rode past on a stolen horse from a fallen paladin. He intercepted their clash, cleaving Wellington's arm, leaving him face down in the dirt by the roadside.

Krell turned to the twins yelling, "FLY, PRETTY BIRD! FLY OR DIE!"

Kat didn't want to. Not when Krell had offered her revenge, face down in the dirt. Wellington's life was ripe for the taking.

Catherine grabbed her by the arm, "Gaffer didn't die so we could follow."

"I'll worry about that once I've dealt justice and honoured Gaff," Kat spat.

"You want to honour him? Then do as he commanded. Run!"

Kat looked at her reflection again, this time shown in Catherine's tears. Her smile had died, and Gaffer's blood lay atop the others. All of his vitality and being was sprayed over her face, dripping from her hair, and down between her bosom. A bad end for a good man.

With the utmost resentment, Kat left the battle with her sister, and disappeared over the valley's horizon. They headed north, away from Valordolt and the savage might of the Order.

Chapter 6: Burnout

Ash was torn, his body cut apart by blades of all kinds, and his will severed from his mind. Vipsa had fallen, as had Gaffer. Now Opyus and Krell were all that remained of his army.

He and Opyus were back to back, systematically picking off anyone that came close. It was all for naught, as for every fallen paladin, another one was there to take its place.

Wellington was a thug, but a thug with respect, he rallied hundreds for the slaughter. There was no end in sight. With a spearhead broken off into his guts, twisting them into a fleshy amalgamation of pain, Ash couldn't fight anymore; he was done.

Keeling over with blurred vision, he watch Krell ride a red-soaked horse around the macabre valley. Opyus took an arrow to each knee, and Wellington rose from the mud, cleaner than when he fell, with Gaffer's spilled blood now concealed by brown grime. James was breathing, but lay motionless by the cobble, his stone skin cracked and chipped away, the Time Stone still remaining around his neck.

The pain was overshadowed by a feeling of failure, emphasised by the horrified traders, watching from atop the valley. From crying girls to disappointed merchants, they saw only one thing in Ash: a villain.

Among the crowd was a person who didn't seem all there. They were suited in jester's attire, waving an emerald gemstone in the air while making rude gestures with their other hand. With a face concealed by a white, smiling mask, Ash had no idea whether man or woman lay beneath. Only one being could be so brazen: the dreaded Trapmaster.

Hericore's plan was over before it began, and the mind-manipulating Master knew this. Ash was mocked for a few more moments, before reality returned. In a blink of an eye, Ash's vision cleared and the Master was gone.

With fleeting lucidity, he watched Opyus stand over him, offering a final request to his boss. Ash's heart shuddered at that title. He hadn't earned it, not now. His first mission as leader, and it ended with his end – hardly a victory.

"The black knight, sir, he's still coming. You need to leave... I'll hold him off," Opyus offered, but it was an offer he needed to refuse.

"I can't," Ash blurted. "The Stone..." Though Mind was out of reach, Time still needed to be protected. He slowly crawled towards the fractured gem, determined to be its saviour, even if he couldn't say the same for his team.

"I'll get the Stone, but right now, you're what matters," Opyus insisted, with an honest look of heroism.

"I failed the mission. They're all dying."

"But *I* haven't failed. My mission, as a soldier and a healer, is to keep my commander safe. Now leave!"

"I can't–"

"You can! It's just like charging into battle, only in the other direction," Opyus said kindly. "There's no dishonour in wanting to live."

If Ash hadn't been broken, he wanted nothing more than to shake Opyus' hand. The old molluskan was truly noble. Ash couldn't claim the same.

Running was excruciatingly painful; every stretch of every muscle was a dagger in his body. All he could do was power through the stabs and never look back.

Krell rode around him, for a time, before redirecting himself at James' body, leaving Ash to escape alone. A wolf in exile.

"Let's see. Who's next?" Wellington questioned as he searched what remained for his next victim. "Ena, mena, mona, mite-" he rhymed, before immediately fixing onto Opyus, "-my old pal 'Pyus is caught in my sight."

The molluskan didn't humour the mad dog's bloodlust. Throwing down his sword, he yelled for mercy.

"It's your job to honour the Order's code and its preservation of life. You can't kill me," the molluskan informed him.

"Because you've always honoured the code, *traitor*." The last thing Ash saw of the old fish was Wellington bringing down his bastard blade on the poor ganger, before issuing a challenge. "You best run, dwarf! But good luck hiding!"

Ash did just that, and carried his wounded self away from the battle, cleaving down one last paladin in his escape – a young lad, who could barely hold his shield. All the carnage was of no consequence, not when his mind was so full of guilt, guilt not just from cowardice, but for abandonment. He'd left Opyus, James, even the dead-headed Krell, all because he was their leader and had the luxury to do so.

With the Time Stone captured, and everyone else dead or missing, he'd lost the battle with the Order's might. But the war wasn't over. If he could reach Rysin's Roost, friends still resided there, he had a chance to pull the mission back from the brink.

Such a wondrous redemption proved near impossible. His lower wounds were warm, and leaked out all manner of fluids. His sprint turned to a run, and the run slowly decelerated into a walk. In the end, Ash was reduced to crawling across a ploughed field, the sound of horses crying and men yelling dropping out of the air, and soon a peaceful quiet was all that remained.

"At least I'll make good fertiliser for whatever farm I'm lucky enough to die on," he said, with a melancholy expression.

For Ash, his journey had reached its end. The warm wounds festered further, no longer having the effort to ache. Making matters worse, he'd travelled so far from the fight that he was disorientated, and collapsed on his back. It was over.

"Dammit! Didn't think I'd go like this. Murder would be a mercy."

Then the rain started up again, pouring on the dying fighter. The storm washed away the bad smell of his oozing wounds, bestowing on Ash one last moment of peace, despite how elemental it was.

The happiness of one's death relied on the quality of one's life. Ash had lived a good life, for the most part: a lengthy affair, it was once full of family and love, but not anymore.

"First Gaffer, now me. Us dwarves are dropping like flies. Guess it's up to you now, Harlan. Make me proud, pal. Save this gods-forsaken planet," Ash said, agitated by the end. "Molly, my legacy is in your hands now, baby girl. I know not where you call home, but I'm smiling... smiling for you, kiddo."

He lost consciousness, and let go of all his pain and ache in one instant, moving on to a better place – to Etheriam. The last thing he heard was the sloshing of water, followed by a faint, familiar voice.

"Father?"

Chapter 7: Sitting in the Cinders

K at escaped the Order, night passed her by, and when light returned, the Gangers were in complete dismay.

She and Catherine found refuge near an old riverbed, hugging the edge of a dead woodland near Valordolt. The two sat apart near the bed, surrounded on both sides by bushes and withered trees, both grieving over Gaffer's sacrifice. They both took the harrowing tragedy in vastly different ways.

Catherine had never lost anyone before, and was almost renewing the old river with her constant streams of tears, which ran unrecognisable from the droplets of rain across her face.

Kat was much more resistant to the emptiness. She remained hardy, distant too, caring more about the principle of letting Gaffer die, rather than the actual thought of never seeing the old dwarf again. Catherine had removed her glamour hours ago, and was sporting her normal face once more. It was a shame Gaffer couldn't see it before he died.

But Kat refused to reveal her face. The stranger's face she wore, was all she had to motivate her – to lose Helena's face was to lose her lust for the fight.

The two didn't have a plan. They waited and waited by the river for something to happen, cats without an owner.

"We can't sit here forever," Catherine said, wiping away her sorrows.

"Just watch me," Kat replied, determined to outlast the wind and rain. But her sister didn't bend so easily.

"Bridgeport can't be more than a day or two away. If we-"

"No. I'm staying put."

Catherine was new to grief – she didn't understand the complexity of moving on. Repression would be her undoing.

"Well, I'm not staying put. I actually want to eat, and sleep, and piss in something other than a shrub."

"You leave now, and Gaffer's death will follow you. When you're eating and sleeping, it'll creep up and crush you. Then, when you think you've forgotten all about it – the exact moment – that'll be when he'll rear his ugly head again."

"I'm not like that. He *won't* follow me." Her sister put on a strong face, but Kat could sense her wavering mind, another solid reflection of her own struggle; they both needed motivation, and soon.

"What would you give to have peace?" she questioned.

"Peace?"

"Yes, peace. Peace from those tears you cry, and the fear of being without a mentor. Peace from last night and ghost that'll follow."

"I don't know. Returning home could be a start."

The west was far away, and its embrace was missed, but the west wasn't going anywhere. Gaffer's honour was torn apart, with the pieces quickly vanishing. If he wasn't avenged *now*, all the crafty dwarf lived for would be gone.

"Wrong! That way to move on is to return the burden to Wellington. To silence the bald bastard – for Gaffer."

Catherine gave her a knowing look. "For Gaffer, or for you?"

"Does it matter?" Kat replied, posing an equally unanswerable question.

Holding little conviction for her motives, Catherine disagreed. "We'd be signing away our lives. Clashing with the Order's militant head would be suicide." Extensive time around Gaffer had made her a beacon of caution over the years, something Kat hadn't adopted.

"As opposed to what? Suicide back in the Wasternlands? We need this... this vengeance," Kat said, in a fiery manner.

"You need vengeance. I need lunch," Catherine sighed.

The fire inside continued, and as with all angered souls, Kat's tongue loosened. Kat did want to make more enemies, but when she'd lose those closest to her, something else was also taken. Gaffer was her rock, and now, going forward, things were crumbling alongside the defeated dwarf.

"You've always undermined my choices, you and Gaffer." Kat lashed out with irate words. "I'm was always the failure when compared to you."

"You're no failure, sis. Just a little set in your ways. And that's okay, but please see reason today. I don't want to crusade for revenge, I want to live," Catherine followed, attempting to comfort her.

It would've been a nice piece of comfort to hear it from Gaffer's mouth, but Catherine would do. For now, Kat held her need for repayment close like a bullet, ready to aim at Wellington when the time was right.

"Live and let live," she said, and achieved a brief respite of peace. Without another word Catherine shuffled over to her sister and held her tight with all the love she had left. It wasn't going to bring Gaffer back, but it did warm the girl's broken hearts.

***

Time passed, and all was well. The bird's chirps in the background and the gloomy clouds above were all Kat had to distract her from the blood on her hands. It was enough, a state of harmony that could hold. This was until a friendly menace appeared from the bushes behind them.

A familiar face, or rather, a familiar mask came stumbling towards them, clutching his bloody axe in one hand, and the priceless, blue stone in the other.

"If things weren't crazy enough?" Kat said, having hazy remorse from the prior night.

Krell didn't respond. Panting and wheezing, he fell down from exhaustion. Judging from his shallow wounds, he wasn't dying, but was lacking stamina, being unable to prop himself up against the tree stump to her left.

"How did he find us?" Catherine said. She perked up and began to scan the woodlands with a cautious eye.

"We can't have left a trail, the Order would've got here first."

Kat came close to the tired warrior, and sat at his side. Krell's tired body was cut and bruised, but in fairly good condition for a man that went toe to toe with fate. The poor thing shuddered from the cold air, and his whimpering managed to reach a place deep within Kat – a place of maternal caring.

"That stone in his hand? It's the one Gaffer had his eyes on," she said, examining the waving ocean of blue inside the gem. Her hand made contact with the alluring crystal mass, and as she did, a wave splashed outward. In the next instant, the wave consumed her body, casting her back – far back.

The stone separated her grief and slashed it around the landscape, replacing the dead wood with the sandy knolls of Diaso. A clear waterfall dripped from the rocks, landing into the pure coastline. Warmth beat down and salt was in the air, wrapping around the small village of huts and hovels – Little Diaso, as she left it. Kat was home.

But the people that faded into view weren't so familiar, all hollow shades moving across the white sands under her feet. Only three people were free from such frail appearance: a young pair of twins and their dwarven guardian.

Gaffer watched the children run circles around a great palm tree, playfully basking in the folly of youth. He looked youthful himself, more than Kat could ever remember. No braided beard covered his blunt chin, and fat hadn't visited his body or limbs.

It was torture to see this vision of days gone by, and another slip of tongue befell her.

"Gaffer?" Kat whimpered, with a bated breath of joy. And in that moment of whimsy, Kat realised, this was no vision.

"Yes, ma'am, that's me. What can I do for a fine lady like yourself?" he asked.

He was talking to her, seeing her. This wasn't her memory echoing back. This was him, the past brought to her on a silver platter. Not knowing how long this would last, Kat threw herself on Gaffer, starting a hug that had to last.

"I'm sorry," she cried, freaking out the baffled dwarf.

For what it was, it was perfect. But all good things died, and that went double for her. In Gaffer's distracted state, the twins' playful laughter was silenced with the drop of a coconut from the palms.

Kat couldn't remember that day very well – not the people nor the mysterious blonde – only the hard crunch of her skull under the force of falling fruit. The pain she felt then reverberated into the present, piercing her brain and snapping her tether to the blue gem, retracting the past.

No, not again. Not again! she repeated to herself, over and over. Eventually, the smells, sounds and feeling of home were gone. Kat started to return back to the chilling present, with empty arms and want.

Disillusioned by the past she couldn't have, one more reality struck. Knowing not of its place in time and space, or even its place as fact or fiction, she welcomed it still. A warm feeling filled her emptiness; a great body able to fill all it touched. This reality was of a great deep, an ocean of black and blue, capable of consuming even her wayward self. Drowning in the abyssal waters was comforting, and Kat finally felt safe.

Chapter 8: Reignition

Zarpadon marched to the south of Prime, his search for answers only half complete, and hoped that Hugo, Patriarch of Mankind, was the missing half.

When Hugo staked his claim in Gideon's world, nobody liked it, and still to this day, he harboured most of the gods' hatred. Not even Hugo knew what caused such a dark arrival in the lands of Prime or why he lacked a form to call his own. But, being ever persistent, like the humans he birthed, Hugo did not surrender to Gideon's rule; instead he cut a large, dark scar on the face of Prime and named it home.

This home, called the Ebone Chasm, made Prime look ugly and tainted from a distance, stretching across several miles of land that once belonged to gods with far more worth than Hugo. Stealing Gideon's face for himself wasn't enough, and Hugo's jealousy manifested a race of his own; a race of shades made in the image of power. Hugo birthed the first humans, never thinking that eventually this race would one day rule the world.

On approach, Ebone Chasm emptied Zarpadon's head of all pre-existing thought, and filled the mental void with the worst kinds of things. What if Hericore was wrong and Zarpadon was backing the wrong horse? Philip could've been right about Sicilla. If Zarpadon had been stronger, would she still be alive?

These bouts of self-doubt passed and returned in more frequent pulses the closer he came to Hugo's chasm, a defence mechanism to thwart intruders. It used fear to invoke cowardice, a far more effective ward than power or want – the tools of Hugo's peers.

Gideon, Theoline, Valentine... all of their powers could never touch the external being that was Hugo, but his influence could reach them, and Gideon's rising paranoia could be a result of keeping Hugo's company far too long. Zarpadon often heard Theoline refer to the Patriarch as a mangy dog, picking what scraps he could off the surface of Prime, being more of a pest than a god.

Ebone Chasm connected the world of Prime to Hugo's domain, a formless land of shadow, made only of pure fear and jealousy. One jump was all it would take for an audience with Hugo, but while he stood on the precipice of the chasm, Zarpadon wouldn't take the dive. It was a leap of faith that a scared man, try as he might, could not make alone.

"I'd advise not jumping if I were you," said a bland voice, unlike his own.

Zarpadon turned to see another crystivine staring at him, one of the enslaved, with no face to tell it apart – only a voice, sharp like daggers, separated this being from any other crystivine.

"And you are?"

"Eight-Four-Two, the one and only servant of Lord Hugo."

"Hugo's servant?" Zarpadon replied. Being the profaned god that he was it was strange Hugo had a servant, even one of crystivine origin. "I seek your master's company, at once."

The enslaved crystivine sat on the edge of Ebone Chasm, feet hanging over the abyss, breeze sweeping across its crystal mass.

"That is not possible. Lord Hugo has disappeared," it said, with an emptiness to its words.

"Let me guess. He disappeared a year ago?"

It paused. "Yes, how did you-"

"I had a hunch. A big, obvious hunch."

History had a knack for orbiting around specific dates and events. The gods' slow crumble was directly related to the Time Stone's own shattering back at Fort Palmer. Lady Palmer, Giovanni, Gideon, Theoline, and now Hugo, a great chain tied to Hericore's curse – a never-ending chain that needed to be unravelled. Zarpadon scoffed at the impossible notion.

"What's down there then?" he wondered, pointing to the chasm. "If it has no master any more, then what lives within?"

"No one has returned from the chasm since Hugo left. Hence my original warning."

A feeling of hopelessness creeped up on Zarpadon and he couldn't help but regret wasting his time back at the Archives. "Then I came all this way for nothing?"

"Maybe not. I have spied a great many things this past year," the other crystivine replied.

"Is that so?"

Whatever crossed Eight-Four-Two's gaze must be of importance. The ever-serving angels had little care for the mundane; a life so long only left room for remembering things of importance.

"The snake dies, then the carrion eaters swoop in for a feast. That is nature at work," riddled Eight-Four-Two. It stood up, back on Zarpadon's level. "When my master disappeared, he was presumed dead by a great many people. And recently, I spotted such a scavenger hoping to pick the corpse of Ebone clean."

"What is there to pick clean around here? All I see are barren fields and misty mounds."

"Yes, that is what litters the land *now*. But before, a great mausoleum was built upon that cliff," Eight-Four-Two told him, gesturing at a corroded cliff opposite them. "Until the crows came to pilfer its secrets."

Snooping souls lurking on Prime wasn't uncommon – Zarpadon was a case in point – but invading the home of a god? That was sinful, unlawful to all mortals, both alive and dead.

"The carrion eater is a god?" Zarpadon asked, confused.

"A rather beloved god, yes. One with the beauty of Valentine, but the hand of Solaris. Bethany is who you seek."

Fear left him at that point, as he knew where to head next in hopes of finding this chain's link. His adventure on Prime wasn't over – not while Bethany remained a suspect.

"Thank you, Eight-Four-Two. I'll be on my way," Zarpadon respectfully said, "and I hope for your master's safe return."

"As do I. A servant without his master is a sorry thing."

It was sad to see his own kind like this, reduced to nothing more than glowing help desks. That wasn't how anything should live. All Zarpadon wanted was to grab its hand, whisk it away from this wretched place, and tell it to never look back.

"Will you return to Magnus?" it asked him.

"Bethany is the next best thing for me right now. She's my only lead and by that logic, Magnus' only hope in uncovering the 'why'."

"The 'why'?" the crystivine wondered, rather inquisitive for an angel. Times changed, as did the curiosity of those enduring it. Eight-Four-Two was a fountain of reminiscence and self-reflection.

Zarpadon nodded. "Yes. Why the world is dying. I need to-"

But before he could finish, the mute servant Cait came into view. She must've followed in his tracks since his meeting with Theoline. She had a message orb in her hands and a sad look on her face.

Taking the orb from her, news from Theoline poured forth; news he could've done without hearing.

"Zarpadon, I can't see much anymore, you know this. But I have seen something dire in Ester Valley. Your friends, they're dying – all of them. Your little games have turned awry, and now not even the vultures will feed on them," Theoline's message warned, reigniting the fear within Zarpadon. "I know you seek knowledge. I do also. But friends can mean more than any piece of information. I only wish I'd treated mine with more care," the message continued.

Whether a trick from his old master – one last joke, or a genuine helping hand, he couldn't turn down the safety of his men. Returning the orb to Cait, he gave her one last reassuring stare, and prepared to leave Prime, for what he hoped to be the last time.

"I must go, my people need me," he told Eight-Four-Two. "You should come too. I can show you so much more than an abyss."

If Eight-Four-Two had a face, it'd would've smiled – Zarpadon could tell.

"I can't. I was made this way. I must serve to my last day."

It was a hard life to live: being a fallen angel wasn't a life for everyone. Zarpadon just wished he didn't have to brave it alone.

With Prime behind him, a beam of pink energy slung him back across the universe to Magnus, and freed his mind from fear, knowledge and the gods.

***

Dropping back on Magnus' soil, Zarpadon landed close to Ester Valley. A light spell of rain trickled down his crystal chest as he desperately wished to find his friends together, victorious.

But he was late to the battle – hours late. The sun was rising high, but shone dimly on The Vitalands, and only corpses of those brave enough to fight remained in the valley. Death's odour hadn't set in yet, only the scent of burning flames and bloody puddles filled the air. Coupled with the moans of the wounded, it wasn't a nice scene to witness.

Peeking over a knoll of torn grass, Zarpadon saw the Order tying up and caging James, along with the molluskan who led the ganger group Vipsa. Both were living, but surrounded by crusaders and rangers, a guard far beyond Zarpadon's arcane capabilities.

Near the newly acquired prisoners, another group were loading up a cart fit to bursting with the dead, all waiting to be buried or burned, depending on the faction they served. The bodies were of the Doppel Gangs, and not of the Drakeguard, which was a relief. Even more importantly, the Time Stone was nowhere to be seen. Ash was doing his job.

Wellington was sitting on the carcass of his dead steed, cleaning his bloody blade. The Battlemaster loved to win, and today was no exception.

A young squire cleaned the panting mad dog's armour, and clerics circled him, healing his cuts and fractures with Bethany's prayers. It was sick to see intelligent men use their talents to fix a monster like Wellington. The brute had dealt more death than his clerics could repay in life.

"Sir, we still can't find the others. They must be hiding in the dead woods," said one of the crusaders.

"Very well. We'll head there now and hunt the bastards down," growled Wellington. "Willy, bring me a new horse and some breakfast."

Before his squire could follow the demand, a wooden carriage, black as the puddles thickening around it, came riding into the valley from Valordolt. It was heavily protected, with resplendent silver knights keeping it out of harm's way; men of the Casterlands serving an Order carriage. It slowed at Wellington's feet, and a withered face poked out from its window.

"You look thoroughly foiled, love. Care for some tea?" asked Dirk, pulling her old mouth back into a smile.

"I'm busy," Wellington replied with a dismissive attitude. The Battlemaster had an iron resolve in all walks of life, countered only by the rustic scorn of a hag like Dirk.

Dirk scoffed. "Too busy licking your wounds? Last chance for tea."

"Tea's for the weak. I need a beer."

"Well, I can't help you there, kid. Haven't touched the bottle for decades. My drunkard days pre-date your birth, no doubt," Dirk said, with a little tinge of nostalgia.

With a punch to the earth, Wellington told of the Drakeguard's great ruse, a ruse they'd thought to be unnoticeable.

"The bastards were using Gangers to fool us. Philip, Helena, Travis... all of 'em were fakes sent to distract us."

"None of them were real?"

"James here is, couldn't find a medium on him. Maybe Ash, too, but he ran. Won't have gone far – messed him up summin' bad."

"Leave him. We have this one to tell us everything," Dirk said, looking at James and harbouring sadistic intent. "You'll take him to Bridgeport and perform his 'interrogation' there."

"But Ash-"

"If you 'messed him up' as well as you claim, he is a dead dwarf walking. We need information on what Hericore's planning and the dead don't talk."

Even after a night of battle, Wellington was sharp as his blade. "You all right, Ms. Dirk? Never seen you so interested in my work."

"This isn't your regular band of crooks. Hericore's was a great leader once. The disillusioned drake will probably do himself in before we can, but I'm not a risk taker," Dirk said, and daintily slipped her tea between each statement.

"Why? Hart's already tracking down the others," Wellington huffed lazily.

"And you trust our warden? His revenge can't be quelled, and if Porter is south, that's all he'll be going for – revenge."

Zarpadon was troubled with how much they knew of the plan already. Someone must've been a mole from day one for them to know so much. That, or someone didn't make it out of Valordolt.

"If Hart's such a problem then why did ya let him leave?"

"I have agents lingering. They'll sort out any problems that arise in the south. All you need to worry about now is that orc and what he knows," Dirk replied. Looking back to Valordolt on the horizon, she adopted a spark of patriotism. "Try as he may, Hart's anger won't sit in my Order."

"Your Order? I've as much of a claim on it as you," contested the Battlemaster.

"Yes, but you lack a certain – *je ne sais quoi* – some say it's brains and other say patience, I believe it's both my dear," she reasoned. "We need each other to stand upright. That's how the pillars of Valordolt work."

Hericore had abandoned the Order for a single day, and already those who remained were busy warring in the resulting power vacuum. Then again, Hericore left his seat of Arch-Paladin long before the breakout, leaving a far greater void that was filled with the greed of others.

"Whatever. If this means less paperwork, then I don't care who runs this shitshow," Wellington said carelessly.

"I'd watch that tongue. Bethany saved your hide last night. I for one think she deserves some respect for it," Dirk scolded. "I've already had to deal with Clara's mood swings; I don't need your foul words too."

"How's the girl doing? She looked as if she'd half a mind to toss herself down the apples and pears."

"She'll live, but has her disbeliefs. Thinks she can't fill Seb's shoes."

"Damn right she won't fill his shoes, the bloke was four times her size." A jape flatter than Wellington's head came as no surprise to Dirk. She didn't bat an eye at the poor joke and continued to slip her drink.

"*Hilarious,*" she sighed. "Now get back to work. Time to earn more of Bethany's fair favour."

The real hilarity lay in Dirk's self-serving lies. The Order's victory didn't hinge on the favour of a god, but a god's favour did hinge on the victory of the Order.

Zarpadon had heard enough, and waiting so close to the embers of conflict was a death sentence; he needed Ash, and he needed the Time Stone. With the wilted woodland behind him, he decided it'd be the best place to start. Ash was maybe up in Etheriam now, and it was up to the fallen angel to pick up his mantle.

***

Zarpadon's near endless searching paid off when the crazed screams of Krell echoed around the hollowed woods. In the time he'd spent with Krell, never had a scream been so vicious, directed at a point of raw concern for the madman.

The crystivine moved through the underbrush, arriving at a dried-out river where Krell and the twins were camped. It was unburdening to see them safe. The pair were young and didn't deserve to be another tally on Wellington's death count.

Though safe from Wellington, they found themselves in a spot of bother with Krell. The psycho had a firm grasp on Kat's neck, as she rested unconscious in his hands. Catherine stood back, yelling at Krell, while pointing an unloaded crossbow at him.

"Have I missed something?" Zarpadon asked, making a rapid approach.

"You've got some timing, angel. Tell this slab of meat to back off from my sister!" Catherine ordered.

"What did she do?" he asked.

"Hell if I know. She touched that rock, then she disappeared. When she came back, Krell launched at her."

Mustering all the discipline he could, Zarpadon hollered a mighty restraint at his watchdog, one learned from an unusual young dandy.

"Krell, yield, you naughty boy! I am *very* disappointed in you." This trick had saved his life long ago, and to this day, it still baffled him how much control Philip had over Krell's broken mind.

Luckily, the verbal leash worked, and the psychopath regressed into a state of internal struggle. Kat was freed, and tended to by her worried sister. She was a little blue in the face, but she wasn't going to die. After a never-ending day of trial, Zarpadon stopped, sat, and allowed himself the treasure of rest – if only for a few minutes.

Krell calmed in time, becoming quiet and isolated from the world around him. He'd often whisper chants in a foreign tongue, some elvish, but many melded with the gruffness of orcish. Try as he might, Zarpadon couldn't decipher the solitary thoughts of Krell.

"What is that thing?" Catherine asked, pointing at the Time Stone, still stiffly held in Krell's grip.

"That's the reason we keep fighting."

"Gaffer used to tell me fairy tales of mystic magic, time travellers, and vanishing vixens. Claimed he saw one such wanderer himself. They can't be real, can they?"

"Bibles are nothing but fairy tales, but it doesn't mean the gods aren't real." Zarpadon said this with slight disbelief, possessing the knowledge of Theoline's recent admissions. After all the lies, could the gods hold any real power, or was it all an illusion?

"Fairy tales, really?" groaned Kat in disbelief, waking from her breathless state.

"Welcome back, traveller," Catherine joked. Hugging her breathless sister, a shallow question soon lea to a far deeper answer. "Visit anywhere nice?"

Zarpadon's last trip in time sent him to a millennium past. It was a surreal experience, and he could only wonder where Kat ended up.

"I saw *him*. I saw us. We were so young," Kat said, sounding deeply depressed.

"No, you can't have..." Catherine said, matching her sister's sad tone. "Gaffer?"

"Clearly you two had a horrid night," Zarpadon said, noting the absence of their dwarven friend.

"Ain't that the truth," Kat said, her blank face a testament to the family she'd lost.

"For your loss back there, I apologise. My friends have perished too, I suspect."

The sacrifices of the lost couldn't be overlooked. He remembered the past, but never let it cloud his future. If Ash died, if Gaffer died, it wouldn't be for nought.

"We're trying to avoid talking about it. Last thing we need is to get emotional now and do something stupid."

"Better now than later," Zarpadon said, changing the subject. "We should move on-"

"In more ways than one," interrupted Catherine, reversing the talk, unwilling to move on either.

"-I doubt the Order will skip this place while searching. We need to move." Kat didn't respond immediately. She just lingered on the Time Stone, fixed on its lustre.

"Can I go back again and see Gaffer? One last time, one more goodbye."

"The Stone is powered by a source we don't possess. That was your last goodbye." Zarpadon denied her, being purposely vague about the workings of the Stone. If she knew of its workings, she'd slay the planet for a thousand farewells.

"Then where can we go? All the nearby towns are operated by the paladins," asked Catherine.

In Zarpadon's eyes, James was the next target, but he couldn't do it alone. Broken or not, the twins would be a great help.

"I have an old friend up in Bridgeport. He owes me a favour. We can't be less than a few miles away, and could make it by tomorrow. From there I can help you reintegrate with society, free from the Order's grasp."

This was a half-truth. Yes, he had a friend in Bridgeport, but it would impossible to help the girls lose their soaring notoriety at this point. They were all wolves in poorly-stitched sheep's clothing. They debated this course of action between themselves for some time, a debate thick with talks of the west and of fairy tales, eventually coming to a sound agreement.

"Despite my objections, we'd be happy to join you," announced Kat. She then reached out her hand. "Put 'er there, boss."

"Zarpadon. Just, Zarpadon," he replied, shaking her dirty hand, coated with flakes of dried blood. "Come on, Krell. We've got work to do," he said, as the new team headed north to the riverside city of Bridgeport. The angel without a home was leading demons without a cause.

Chapter 9: A Fool's Petard

Donsis had severed the last leg he stood on, and now sat alone in his old cell, while Rangar roamed the green forests, free. The view Donsis had was less idyllic – grey clouds, factory smoke, and the damp streets outside of Refracted Light.

Regret overflowed the bounds of his being, and after suffering the slurs of common folk, this regret extended to deeds far before his imprisonment. Every dwarf he'd spat on and all the humans he'd lugged in with them came back to haunt the elf. He didn't need to be caged in a cell to know he was an animal.

All that remained now was Hart's pardon, the one act that could save him from execution. The executioner was gone, but the Order very much wanted to kill someone over the night's events. They lost a lot of good men, and a few bad too – not that they'd mention that little detail.

Donsis escape from the statue had been a close one. The ringing still caused his head to ache, but that was it. Thanks to the weird words of an even weirder stranger, he'd dodged death another time, tallying up to an innumerable amount.

The cut on his hand was festering with no visible ailment, but on the inside it burned like the clap. Why he'd not fallen to the effects of the blade yet were unknown, and he didn't care. Kalsec was a stranger now, and whatever curse he carried wasn't in effect yet.

"That's not going away," whispered a voice from beyond the iron, cell door. It was so distinctive that Donsis identified it without a second thought.

"Kalsec! Praise Aldon you're here."

"Don't be too grateful; I can't stand being praised. I just stopped in to say 'hello'. Finding a guard's armour wasn't easy, so I'll make this quick. Your days are numbered, elf. But you could help me in your last moments."

"What happened to being strangers? My life isn't over. Hart will pardon me any minute now."

But the title of 'Suicidal Skelly' was a hard one to shake. The memories of Trawlers' would stick around forever. Doubting one's actions was a poor course of action. Never entertaining the past for more than a moment, Donsis looked to the future, a future Hart was holding the keys to.

"That sounds peachy keen: rat out your friends and earn a pardon. If only..." doubted Kalsec. Something about the man sounded different: something was missing. He felt like a stranger to the elf.

"You disappeared and left me to the wolves. I'm not helping you. Hart will pull through," Donsis said confidently.

"I'm sure he will. And I'm sure whatever I did to you was just. I only want to know one thing. When you met me and I branded you, did I give you a message? A code, perhaps?"

Six-Three-Six was the only odd thing he'd parted with last night. The gent's inability to recall it was actually amusing to Donsis; even the calm and collected sort forgot things from time to time.

"It was last night. How can you have such a poor memory?" Donsis teased.

"Just spill it, rat. I'm tired of hearing you speak, especially in a tone so mocking. I need to know."

Unsettling wasn't the word; with a sheet of iron between them, Donsis wasn't even convinced it was the same man he'd met in Trawlers'. After a night of mayhem, anything could be in Kalsec's place.

Donsis set his jaw. "Look elsewhere. As I recall, you think of me as a burden, and nothing more. I'm happy keeping my maw shut this time."

"Happy, but not safe," seethed the stranger, stabbing his sabre right through the inches of iron, narrowly missing the elf's head. "My next stab won't miss."

Hanging cells were small, and the sabre could pierce right though from one end to the other. With the sabre dripping with fresh blood, there was no doubt that its wielder cared little for life. Compliance was almost a compulsion for Donsis.

"Okay, I'll tell you, I'll tell you. You said 'Six-Three-Six.' Six-Three-Six."

A long pause raised tensions, only to have them dashed by a sinister but happy laugh.

"Ha, really? That explains the papers. I suppose I could add 'Belmont Bomber' to my list." Sounding rather proud, the gent's metal heels clopped all the way down the hall. "Ta-ta, elf."

"It's 'Donsis," he reminded. "Let's hope you remember this time."

Unable to make head nor tail of the elusive gent, Donsis rested his head against the door, and for the first time all day, doubted Hart's promise. A flash of blue blasted through the hole in the door, and Kalsec's metal boots stopped smacking the floor.

Before Donsis knew it, the door swung open, and his rest was broken. Falling face first onto the cold floor, his sore head took a second beating. Standing over him was Lud, a brute with little sense of sympathy for the elf's fall. Pulling him by the shoulder, two words barked from Lud's lips.

"Move it!"

After his last heart-pounding visit, Donsis just wanted to rest, but the wicked had no such opportunity.

"Did Hart request this? Because I expected a bigger escort," he asked, thinking of Kalsec once more. "A lot of people want me dead."

"You give yourself too much credit, loan shark. I'll manage," said Lud, forcing him out of the chilly room into the equally cool corridor to the rusted iron exit.

On the journey to the central building Donsis noticed a large squad of men loading up carts and packing overloaded boxes of supplies. The trip south was imminent, and judging by the amount of food and horses, over fifty men were going to pursue the prisoners. For the first time since his escape, Donsis felt a calmness about being safe inside prison and not on the receiving end of Hart's sharp personality.

None of the soldiers paid him any mind, which the elf found odd; this late in his life, it was apparent that most, if not all people abhorred him. Boris was just the first of a long list of people he'd wronged in his years of loaning. Breaking legs got results, but some legs were just too risky to break after a while.

"Are you also heading south, or will you stick with me?" Donsis asked, but Lud remained silent.

The security around Central had improved dramatically since the escape, and Donsis finally received many hateful comments from the extra staff, forced into their new posts at the squalid prison. The doors also seemed to be upgraded with reinforced locks, some even rigged with electrone crystals, able to fry any intruder trying to force them. The change appeared frivolous, as Hart's last breakout had come from within; shock locks meant nothing to those with a key.

The upper floor was converted into a sick bay to house the ones unlucky enough to survive an encounter with Hericore's rising army. Some were scorched by fire, others covered in bilious, green skin, welting from poisons. But the most tragic were the survivors with missing parts, lacking full form, not fit for Etheriam's pools.

If the sickly sight wasn't enough, the smells of dead, rotting meat filled the air once dominated by healing scents of many kinds, like the tang of peach or the sting of mint.

"You look surprised," Lud said, "What's got a heartless skeleton like you all shook up?"

"I didn't think so many people would live; after the battle, that is," Donsis said. It was an eerie scene to look over, with nearly a dozen torn and broken paladins being treated by frantic clerics.

"That's what so called 'heroes' like Hericore don't understand. When they go swaggering off after the fight, it's our job to stick the wounded," explained Lud, with disgusted remorse.

"Stick the wounded?" Donsis asked.

"Think that bloke there's gonna survive two snapped legs and a caved skull? Nope. Hart will have to put him down like a sick pup, then add him to the list of black letters to write."

Black letters were apologetic letters sent to the families of dead paladins. Wellington and Hart would've written hundreds of these over the years – never an easy job, and something Donsis was glad he didn't have to endure.

In all his years of vile deeds, he'd refused to loan to friends and those close to him. The last thing he needed was to make a choice between greed and love, because greed would win every time.

Jelz and Boyd were waiting outside Hart's office too. Jelz was clutching his damaged shoulder from a recent skirmish at the gates, and although he claimed to have won, the cracks in his shell said otherwise. Boyd was busy scrawling down some last minute supply requisitions for the upcoming trip; Donsis kept to himself as the oaf made a mess of the form with illegible writing.

Boyd was a long-term member of the Order. Around the same time Hart had started, Boyd graduated as a rookie and soon found himself serving the prison and its warden. Donsis first met Boyd at one of the Order's charity galas, and never understood why the man always looked over his shoulders and shook with every passer-by. Donsis was a coward, but even he found Boyd too superstitious.

Feeling a sense of safety after backing up Hart, Donsis smiled at the two captains, awaiting his meeting with the Warden. Boyd returned the gesture, one of weaker pleasantry, while Jelz ignored the elf and looked away.

During his wait in the toasty offices, Donsis watched Lud's words unfold as one of the wounded paladins started to convulse with rapid seizures – the end was near for the devoted man.

"Hold him," Lud commanded the clerics, pulling an iron dagger from his pocket. "I'll handle this one."

The cleric's oaths swept to the old, armoured man's side, whispering false hope into his ear. With words like '*you fought well*' and '*it'll be over soon*', Lud made sure to plunge the blade into his heart, quick and arguably painless.

Piercing the heart was a standard end for a member for Bethany's following, a sign of sacrificed love in her name. The elder warrior died a good death.

"We've got another fallen fighter!" Lud called to Hart, who was still embroiled by the confines of ink and paper.

"Who?" Hart called back, not leaving the room.

"Cordell... Senior."

"Hells, when will it... Bury him, now! And send 'em all in, both Donsis and my no-good captains."

The three entered, and Lud took the old-timer away. The younger man in a nearby cot had an arrow in his foot and a now a pain in his heart at the loss of the elder – they must've been close.

The office hadn't changed much since the elf's last visit, save for the newly installed coat hooks on the wall and a broken safe near the back. Most the heat was originating from this room, seemingly from a furnace that used anguish as its kindling. It made his cheeks redden in time.

Hart looked undead, with bagged eyes, a pale, faint look, and pints of expended coffee mugs littered around the jittering mess of a man. His jacket was on the floor, as was his iron vest; beside them was a broken portrait of a family, all their faces destroyed. After the attack, a metal brace held Hart's right leg in place; this made walking an even greater challenge thanks to the caffeine causing it to shake uncontrollably.

Coffee was a foreign commodity that Donsis despised in both taste and principal, breathing life into the squalor-stricken folks of the Swallows. He made sure to turn his nostrils up at the pungent brew.

Hart was writing black letters and placing them in an uneven pile on his desk, murmuring every syllable he commemorated to paper. He hadn't appeared to have changed his clothes since last night and gave off a bad smell of sweat and caffeine, with his smart hair losing its sanity; the warden was breaking down, piece by piece.

Hart looked at him gazing at the coat hooks.

"Have you never seen a coat hook before, Donsis?"

"Of course I have. But I'm wonder why you need three. You only wear the one jacket, and it's residing on the floor."

"You wouldn't understand. Even if I told you the answer, you wouldn't accept it," Hart said, in words shakier than Donsis'. "Anyway, that's not why you're here."

"Right, my pardon."

Hope of legitimised freedom, or what could be considered 'free' compared to a lethal alternative, grew inside the elf. If Hart was honest, then all would be well.

"Ah, ah, not yet. Boyd first, then Jelz, then you. Rank before reason," said Hart. His speech was speedier than his normal chilling pattern.

"Thank you, boss," said Boyd. The captain who'd overseen Donsis recent execution, before the Drakeguard stepped in, Boyd was a failure in most ways, yet there he stood, head of the journey south. "We need some more jerked beef for the trip. Problem is, we're close to hitting our budget."

"No matter. By the time Dirk realises we've overspent, we'll be halfway across Midgartt. Spend away. Buy an entire cow if it pleases you," said Hart, continuing to write his letters of death.

Glancing at them, Donsis saw the callous way in which the Warden expressed his condolences. Each sentence of thick lettering was short, snappy, and lacking sympathy for the dead. Hart was pushing for quantity when creating these farewells.

"Of course, boss." Boyd moved back against the wall, giving the others the floor, and Jelz was more than happy to take his place.

"I've received a report on Wellington's movements, sir. He has proven victorious against the Gangers, but refuses to return until all its members are accounted for."

"Well, he'll be gone for a while. We made sure of that, didn't we, Donsis?" replied Hart, with a deep chuckle.

"Heh, yeah," Donsis said nervously, implementing his own, shallow laugh. Looking back, lying before Bethany seemed heretical, even for him.

"Also, if the rumours ring true, then Hunter eviscerated a man during Donsis' capture last night," Jelz added.

Hart stopped writing, looked up, and smiled. Seeing the Warden smile was as uncommon as a laugh. It seemed the recent carnage was coaxing out a buried part of the old veteran.

"Best news I've had all day. We can expose Hunter for the cocky little boy that he is. I want you to bring this rumour to Dirk's desk before we head out."

Jelz looked uneasy. "I can try. The Banker has been in a sleepless state, much like you. The old bat is making-the-rounds across the Vitalands as we speak. Seems an attack so close to home has gotten her little heart a-beatin'."

Finally Hart turned to Donsis, who was standing at the centre of the small room, in front of the desk. The Warden was twiddling a pen between his fingers, completely removed from his writing; he wanted to give Donsis his full attention.

Slowly, and with full attention, a question was passed to him. "Was it worth it?"

"Betraying the only people to ever lend me a hand? I'm still deciding,"

Donsis answered, with his regret showing.

"I was betrayed once, but only the once. With that in mind, I'm afraid there has been a change of plan, Donsis."

In an instant, the elf was robbed of the hope that once oozed in pints. Hart had no right to do this; it wasn't dutiful or fair.

"I did everything you asked. I trusted you, Warden, please," he whimpered.

"Trust that was firmly placed, but a thing I could never reciprocate. I know you were complicit in the Belmont Bombing, and I can't let that slide. My side is still numb from a crashing statue – one you managed to miraculously avoid. Tipped off by your saviours, were you?"

Donsis shook, but not with fear. The finger pointing was too much. First he was a racist and bigot, then a 'skelly', now a slayer of the innocent. Anger and sorrow fought internally, as he tried to toughen up and tell the Warden exactly what he thought. If he was to be executed, then he no longer needed restraint.

"Men like you are some work, Hart. You use the whole 'wounded warrior' routine to make those around you all sympathetic, but underneath the false emotion is *nothing*! A void of sinister plots and manipulative tendencies! I'll be damned if I'll let that continue, you psycho! I'm not letting you kill me!"

Boyd and Jelz smirked behind him, giving each other a look of feigned terror. Once the red in his face faded, Hart continued his speech.

"Jumped the gun there, Donsis. I was going to say that your execution has been halted."

"What?" he gasped.

"You, as in Donsis Allisteel, will not have your head removed from your body... Cristel wants me to question you over the bombing. Apparently you're too important to kill-" With a small, victorious jig, the elf apologised for his crude words, and thanked Hart for this accomplishment. "You have a poor knack for allowing me to finish my sentences," Hart added.

Donsis looked contrite. "I'm sorry, Warden. Please continue."

Hart stood up and braced himself for a wave of negativity. Much like Boyd and Jelz, it seemed a feigned gesture of regret.

"True, I stopped your beheading. However, I must regretfully tell you: your death is destined."

"I'm sorry, but what?" Donsis spluttered.

"People want you gone around here: I do, as do the soldiers, the families of the dead... hell, even the murderers and rapists in the cells hate you," Hart said, tainting the light mood. "That's not to mention that papers and court hearings Cristel wants would waste valuable time. Time I could spend chasing down Kenneth. *Sorry*, Donsis."

The insincere 'sorry' crushed all light left for him. All his life amounted to was more time on Hart's clock – an inconvenient existence.

"But you said you'd help me if I lied for you," Donsis choked, swallowing too much sorrow.

"I did. But I didn't specify how far I could go in helping you," said a stern Hart. "If only your friends hadn't gone a blown half of the Citadel sky high... A quick, quiet death is all the help I can offer."

Clutching his cursed hand, Donsis vowed that he wasn't going down this time. In pain and still reeking of the sewers, humiliation and suffering weren't threats to him anymore. All that remained was to conquer the threat of death; a task he underwent, despite his fears.

"That's not fair. I've changed my mind and don't want to die. Please, you can do this. You're a man of integrity, a man of vitality, you can't..."

Spitting his words, Hart had heard enough uncooperative talk.

"Stop whimpering and accept something for once. You and your criminal friends brought this on yourselves. Paladins have died, civilians too."

"How can I be held accountable for the bomb? I had nothing to do with-"

"Even if you didn't, you're not in the clear," Hart snapped. "Because of your antics at the pub, and your pals' antics at the gates, I'm stuck filling out two-dozen death records for my fallen men, in addition to all the damages." At that point, the captains moved closer to him, ready to act on their warden's word. "Furthermore, I've also got to write up the black letters to the families of the dead. So thanks for that."

"I had nothing to do with the gate. This is unfair. I have rights," Donsis whimpered.

"Unfair, yes. My problem, no." Hart looked at him bluntly, then returned to the letters. "And as for your rights? Your deeds have made them worth next to nothing. As is the way of life. Take him away, boys."

Donsis didn't want to give up any more. His brief taste of freedom had given him hope, a hope to live, that he wasn't about to lose again. Hart had crushed his light, but elves were always good at living in darkness. The Warden's accusatory attitude wouldn't best him.

Taking all of his inner fear and stress, Donsis concentrated it into a moment of pure drive and carelessness, charging directly at the Warden, and disregarded the consequence. He felt the two captains try to hold him back, but it wasn't enough. Grabbing Hart's pen straight from his tired hands, Donsis shouted a feeble war cry. If he was doing to die, Hart join him.

Try as he might, it wasn't enough to even graze the Warden's fine clothing, and several rabid swings later, Donsis had lost his rage. With one clean stroke, Hart disarmed him, let his captains restrain him, then stood level with the elf's face.

"Hold him steady, boys. A little to your right," Hart ordered.

Donsis struggled, but it was a fruitless action. With the end in sight once more, he reverted to his true self.

"I can give you anything. My... my cousin, Yikii, is a wealthy man. He can pay you, I'm sure of it," the elf bargained. Boyd and Jelz's gripped tightened – the restriction was worse than any cell or notion of prejudice.

Hart pulled a curved knife from his draw and raised it to Donsis' thin throat.

"See, this is why I despise you, Donsis. Your answer to everything is *money, money, money*. You never think there's anything else to desire in this world."

"Then what do you desire? I know who bombed the tower: a man named Kalsec. He was here earlier and last night. He's the one who told me to jump left! Please, you've got to believe me," he ratted out. But Hart didn't acknowledge the name, too focused on ending this little meeting of theirs.

The Warden came in close, resting his forehead on Donsis'. With closed eyes he said, "Oh, poor, Donsis. Poor dumb, defenceless, *dead* Donsis. All I want from you is your cooperation in this endeavour."

The Warden coiled back, before kicking Donsis out of his captains' hold, flinging him across the room and spearing the elf's neck straight through the brand new coat hooks.

"Another convenient reason why extra hooks can come in handy, no?" the Warden added, with an incredibly sadistic smile.

Donsis tried to flail around, but couldn't. His spine felt empty and his limbs went limp. Added to this numbness was a large amount of blood spraying out of an open neck wound. It was over.

A life paved with the suffering of others was about to end, and no justice was found in it. Boris' sister didn't revive, the Allisteel wealth rusted in a vault somewhere, and only a broken man was happy.

"Wait, I have an idea," said Hart. "Boyd, take this rodent to Osiris. She will pay well for a sack of flesh and bone like him. Well, sack of bones, anyhow."

Boyd complied and ripped the elf's still breathing body off the hanger with a rather unpleasant crunch.

"Can I have his shoes?" asked the flabby captain, a greed Donsis could appreciate, even in his last moments.

"Fine. This is becoming quite the bad habit of yours."

"What is this?" Jelz asked, with genuine horror.

"Retribution," Hart replied. "You of all people should understand. We're all bad eggs, rotting on the inside. Donsis is just taking a more literal approach."

Donsis lay immobile on the office floor, swimming in a pool of his own blood, and even then, couldn't stop thinking about surviving. He wasn't dying, he couldn't. Denial and doubt followed the elf to the grave.

The happiness of one's death relied on the quality of one's life. Donsis had lived a bad life, for the most part.

Sitting beside him in the blood-soaked office, Hart looked down at the ruined, stained forms and black letters on the desk. Throwing them into the fire, he uttered a simple, "Fuck it."

At least the cursed burning on Donsis' hand had ceased. When life left him, so too did the cut, as if it was never there. All Donsis could think of as he gave up was his now-fulfilled title of 'Suicidal Skelly.'

Chapter 10: *Sori Pec Sori Sann*

Hemora enjoyed a long rest beside his new animal companion, Gerald. If it hadn't been for the rising end of the world, he would have been happy to lie down in this natural serenity forever. He heard the pitter-patter of rain smacking the leaves above him in the forest's dense canopy, but refused to wake just yet.

"A couple more minutes."

Another twenty past, until the smell of petrichor was replaced by the finer sweetness of a bitter, sherbet perfume. But the pleasing scent was soon overpowered by a kick to the side, waking him from his slumber.

From his back, Hemora gazed up and saw Helena standing over him with a scornful look. From the ground, his view was greater than any before, lending a glimpse of the underbust beneath her loose shirt. "Wow, and here I thought you couldn't look any better," he flirted, but was met with disrespect.

"Keep it in your shell, crab. You're lucky to be graced with a view so fine."

Sitting in an upright position, he heeded the friendly advice while readjusting his braces.

"The gods didn't create such a wondrous sight for it to be locked behind the confines of cloth. If you ever bestow that view on me again, I'll be sure to indulge in looking with equal awe."

"Right. Sure," Helena doubted. "I was sent out here to call you back to camp. Hericore was worried you'd leave us, much like Donsis wished."

"No escape from me. What he did was foolish, but I'm a fool of a different kind."

"Then join us for before breakfast, fool, and bring your handsome friend too."

Gerald released a soft snort and jumped in place, kicking up dirt and forcing Hemora away from his new steed's side. In a hasty step back, he fumbled and tripped over the white trunk of a thick birch, causing Helena to make a foreign sound akin to a giggle. Though a deep noise, it was one of joy – the first he'd witnessed from the stubborn gunslinger.

"You're enjoying this too much," Hemora said, stumbling back over the birch stumps.

With his ego deflated, a march back to camp was all he needed. Even at his young age, the day was also young, and as such, made even the most simple of tasks a monumental feat.

"Aren't you forgetting something?" Helena mentioned. Again, she looked over at Gerald.

"Oh, right." He whistled at Gerald. It had no effect. "Move, Gerald, you lazy lump of chow," he complained, with another, stronger whistle. This finally motivated Gerald, and he swished around his shaggy mane, then clopped in circles, stretching out his legs.

"What happened to the owner?"

"Beats me. Victim of a raid mayhaps?"

"Hericore will need to allow his stay in the group. Can't see why he'd turn the big fellah down. If anything, he'll make a good pack mule," Helena remarked, looking the horse up and down with a critical eye.

At the mention of the word 'mule', Gerald gave a look of disapproval to Helena before returning to his exercises through the trees.

"Well, when you're both ready, Harlan's cooking up some mushrooms."

Refusing to wait on the molluskan any longer, Helena moved back toward the camp with a slow and lonesome strut.

"As long as it's not fish, I'm in," Hemora said, gleefully.

Eating fish was of heresy amongst the molluskans of Tealka. Most won't touch the stuff, but many still did, Hemora being part of the former group.

"You don't enjoy the taste?"

"No, I don't enjoy cannibalism," he replied. "I don't carry around human meat with me, so I'd expect the same courtesy."

"That's not quite the same thing," Helena disagreed, before gliding away, past the birch woods. Hemora and Gerald then followed in her footsteps, only at a lazed pace.

Since their liberation from the gloom of Valordolt, the group seemed in a happier and overall calmer state, setting up a fairly large, but concealable place to sleep.

A fire was dug into a dip in the earth, with most of the cowhide bedrolls laid around it, obscuring the whimpering flames. Sitting on the beds were Travis and Lucille, both talking to Hericore about his military days and their mixed adventures across Magnus. From Lucille's hunts to Travis' trip to the Green Isle – a cluster of islands of the coast – no story was the same. All followed a similar narrative – good intentions rusted into dust as the story unfolded.

Currently, it was Harlan's turn to talk, which he accomplished while tending to the weak fire, bolstering its strength with a wave of pyrus-spawned flame.

Rangar sat alone, not too far from where he'd collapsed last night, clutching his now non-existent wound. Travis' divine recovery was in full effect. His other scaly arm hung in a sling, snapped at the joint, limp and useless.

"-and that's when I realised it was *actually* a recipe for shroom stew," boomed Harlan, no doubt a humorous conclusion to a tale long passed, made evident by several laughs.

"They must've been some peeved goblins," Hericore commented.

"Definitely. The greedy wretches wanted the secret to everlasting happiness, and instead they got this thick, albeit tasty, stew." Sticking a finger in the gloop boiling above the fire, Harlan tasted it with pleasure. "Mind you, they're the same thing to me."

Hushing the group upon arrival, Hemora moved to the jolly drake, seeking Gerald's refuge in the Guard's embrace.

"Morning, gents," he welcomed, before turning to Lucille, "and others. Which of you thought it would be fun to jape without me?"

"Hemora, glad you could join us at last. You also have a horse now," said Hericore, pointing out Gerald frolicking in the background. "Huzzah!"

"So he's allowed to stay? Because I'll take responsibility for him."

"Why of course. A horse couldn't hurt our little team."

"Might even be a good replacement for Donsis," called Rangar, from his cosy corner of the camp.

It was an amusing joke that even Harlan found happiness in, not that Rangar presented it as one. It was weird how the previous night's loss was converted to today's mockery. Maybe it said a little much about the company Hemora kept.

"Mushroom stew?" Harlan offered, proud of the soupy creation.

He accepted, and Lucille scooped a ladle of the gloopy, light brown broth into a wooden bowl. It was as Harlan said, thick, with chucks of little fungi swimming about inside the mixture. It looked bad. Its smell contradicted that theory, but he couldn't make any more judgements from appearance alone. The mixture reminded him of a bulb flower, minus the pus glands – though pus seemed to share a consistency with the mix.

Hemora took a sip, and failed to drop dead from poisoning, so overall the soupy meal was passable. With hunger slowly vanishing, he took a seat with Rangar and consoled the pale snake.

"Morning, buddy. You're looking awfully close to shit right now," he said, backing against a mighty oak.

"I take it bedside manners aren't appreciated in Tealka?" Rangar replied, with a limp glimpse of humour on his lips.

"Molluskans love caring for the sick; all of them except me. I never did like hospitals. What's happened to your arm, can Travis fix it?"

"If only. His prayers have trouble breaching my scaly parts. This'll be all natural from here on out. Truth be told, I fight better with one hand."

Hemora continued to evaluate the poor state of Rangar, spying a few long scars across his thick torso.

"And those weren't there before last night. Another rejection from Bethany's mercy?"

"'The flesh will zip right up, but the skin will never heal': the words of a wise man," Rangar said, with remorse for his former aggression.

Honestly, it was an eyesore, only overshadowed by the mass of scales on Rangar's side, warping the flesh around them – the discomfort was palpable, even to him.

"They *do* look hardcore." Hemora lied. "Who knows, maybe you'll attract some women with 'em." Rangar wasn't confident, answering with a heavy exhale of air. "You don't think so?" the molluskan pressed.

"Not at all. I never knew scars were attractive," sighed Rangar. "If I'd known, maybe I'd have lost more fights."

The scaly brute had faced three paladins and won, cementing doubts about whether he could even lose a fight. A man that talented must've earned it: broken men held the shiniest accolades.

"Yeah, the ladies dig scars. Too bad I'd have to shed my shell to show 'em," Hemora said, sharing in the burdened sigh.

"Best hold off on that. Last thing we need is to see your grungy fish junk."

An insult to his face, form, or family was acceptable, but never would Hemora tolerate such an assault on his most precious asset.

"Grungy? I don't think so. I know plenty of lovely elf girls that would swoon over the very thought of my fish junk," he joked.

"Really?" Lucille interrupted. "I'm pretty sure I've never fantasised about the sword you're carrying."

"It's no sword, Lu. Closely resembles my trident. Three tips and everything."

Lucille frowned. "That's not something to be proud of."

"For the record, I'd be proud of that," Harlan added.

Trident was a stretch; the word 'bident' was more fitting. But exaggeration existed for a reason, and Hemora planned to use it.

"Can we stop talking about fish... 'parts'?" pleaded Travis, trying to concentrate on his literature.

"No one's asking you to listen," Rangar said.

"Hard not to."

"See, even you humans can't stop thinking about my trident," Hemora boasted.

"I'm not thinking about your genitals," Travis protested.

"Really? You just said it was hard not to," said Rangar, applying a childish strain of logic. Hemora loved to induce the inner child in the sterner breed of man; they all had it, but many chose to hide it.

"Heh, I bet it's *hard*," said Harlan, as he swooped in with a late pun.

"That joke was some low hanging fruit," Lucille judged, rolling her eyes.

"Yep; low hanging," Hemora said, picking up the mantle of Harlan's innuendo. "Just like my fish-"

"Enough!" said Hericore, stepping in to halt the dark journey the conversation was taking. "The next person who mentions this exchange in anyway will be carrying the entire group's bedrolls for the day."

With this threat in mind, everyone was silenced – for about ten seconds. Hemora couldn't resist the calls of banter for long. It was a second shell to him after years of surfing from pub to pub, staying up late with the local lads – boozing over snoozing, he called it.

"Hmm, this is some great stew, Harlan," Hemora said.

"Well you don't earn the title of 'Midgartt's Greatest Chef' three centuries in a row for nothing," claimed the dwarf. This was a self-proclaimed title, for sure.

"Hmm, yeah, I love how meaty it is..." Hericore looked over at Hemora and shook his head, a warning to stop before it was too late. "Very meaty, like a certain molluskan crotch that I've–"

"I said *enough!*" roared Hericore, as he released a blast of smoke from his nostrils. "Hemora, you're carrying the bedrolls for this day and the next. Maybe next time you'll refrain from trying my orders."

Laughing at the punishment, Hemora simply replied with, "Don't care, I've got a horse now." Gerald accompanied the slick response with a loud whinny of joy, and continued to move around the camp.

Hericore stopped for a moment. A sly look arose on his face with one brow lifting high above the other. As Hericore's brow raised, so did Hemora's terror. What was the drake going to do? Send him back to Valordolt?

"Very well. I can't fault your defiant attitude. But disobey me in the future, and I'll make your punishment so *long* and so *hard...* you could mistake it for your member," the drake promised.

Hemora's face lit up as his entire perception of what he thought Hericore was completely fell apart at the uttering of this promise. The jester was now the jested. It was a scenario so rare, so unpredictable, that the lack of roaring laughter was a compliment.

He looked at everyone, all containing a tsunami of happy shock, then turned back to Hericore, who just waited for the dam of comedy to burst.

When it did, Hemora and Rangar couldn't sit properly, needing each other's support. Lucille spat out a mouthful of hot stew on Travis' extended legs, and Harlan fell in to the fire pit; if not for his pyrus enriched body, he would have burned to a crisp. Hemora hadn't felt this great in years, this group was a bunch of loony clowns, a group that suited his own childish ways perfectly.

Once the laughter turned to tears of wonder and eventually died, they packed up and moved on. Putting another seven miles between them and the Order, they re-deployed their camp under the remnants of an old bridge, which connect two parts of an even older trail through the forest.

Hericore, an even older construct, briefed the Drakeguard on their next goal – Lake Vita, the last landmark the Vitalands had to offer.

"Due to the rain and increase in paladin movement, we're hunkering down here for a few extra hours when the sun rises. Until the storms of water and faith pass us, we need to be quiet, quiet as spirits themselves." A crash of thunder hit the ground to make his stern point a moot one. "Use the weather as a clear example of what *not* to do. Rest up, my friends. Then we move south, free from this downpour."

Having a plan that changed on a whim was becoming commonplace. Hericore was a wise drake, but this didn't make him less flawed than anyone else, just more practised at hiding his flaws from others.

With the prisoners fragmenting into several groups, it was becoming more apparent who was getting friendly with whom, now the dust had settled. Hericore and Harlan's old tales drew in most people, aside from Haruka, who'd remained quiet since leaving Valordolt. She sat on watch, atop the bridge far from Lucille and her new pals – hardly a fun time. Hemora aimed to change this.

She spent her time playing with the red ribbon around her neck, a firm embrace from an inseparable friend. In the evening glow, the ribbon shone bright at angle, catching light and transforming it to a white streak. An ornate ribbon for an ornate girl.

With Rangar by his side, Hemora sat beside her, next to her coldest shoulder, when an impenetrable silence overcame him. Her very nature was a deceptive thing, looking brittle in her isolation, but still so lethal on the inside. She coveted her inner flame, securing it from the chilling world around her, and the molluskan sought to peek at this 'flame'.

"Evening, Haruka. Spy anything interesting from here?" he asked calmly, so as not to aggravate the pint-sized killer.

"Not really. Aside from a couple of ungrateful bitches," she replied, throwing a calm dislike onto those below. "Who does that pampered whore think she is? Getting all chummy with *my* friend?"

Her hatred of Helena was strong, maybe even greater than her concern for her own safety. Making enemies was hard work, a slog that Hemora had never really entertained. Regrettably, others still loved to make an enemy of him.

"We all need to be friends here. Unnecessary dislike will cause trouble when it counts most."

"Unnecessary? What, like starting an argument with me over saving their stupid lives," Haruka furiously replied.

"Admittedly, a crappy move on their part. But you can be the better woman here by making amends."

Rangar joined them on the cold ground, sharing sage-like words.

"If I lost it with Hemora every time he acted like an ass, neither of us would've made it out of Valordolt."

"What? I thought you liked me?" Hemora responded, adopting a fake sense of hurt.

"I do. But I still hate your dumb jokes."

"They are pretty terrible," Haruka agreed.

"See, I don't agree with your opinions, because my comedy strides with leaps and bounds, but I let go and laugh on. This is what I'm trying to preach: friendly banter. It's the happy medium between silent resentment and full blown hatred."

Disheartened, Haruka admitted his point to be a valid one.

"I see what you mean. Doesn't mean I believe it."

"*Yet*. You don't believe it, *yet*," Hemora corrected.

Haruka gave him a thankful, hope-filled smile, and paused before replying to the pair. The raised corners of her lips sunk, then puckered in a concerned fashion.

"Vangesh, we need to talk." She then turned away from Rangar. "In private."

"Why? Whatever you can say to me can surely be told to my better half."

"No, it can't," Haruka frowned. "I know what you are."

It took Hemora a few second to realise what she meant, and if it was what he thought, it was bad news.

"What? What do you mean?" Rangar asked, giving off an air of confusion.

"It's nothing, Rangar, *really*. Just go over there for a minute or two. Let me and Haruka talk it out," Hemora said, in a hushed and defensive tone. But Rangar remained sitting down.

"You can't block me like this, fooling me into believing life's peachy. Nothing is that simple. I promise it'll stay between us."

"This is different. Trust me with this."

His hands shook as he nervously shooed Rangar away with a few flicks of the wrist; this wasn't something he wanted anyone to know, not even a friend. But again, Rangar refused to leave and Haruka couldn't wait any more. After another few rounds of arguing she spilled the beans.

"I know you're a vampire," she whispered, lacking any finesse.

Rangar stopped mid-sentence and looked at him with a raised eyebrow.

"A vampire?"

"Not so loud," he hissed. "Yes, a vampire."

"When were you gonna tell me?"

"I don't know. It's not something you should be proud of. How did *you* know, Haruka?"

With detective like recollection, she listed off the things that tipped her off, a talent Hemora wished she'd pointed elsewhere, rather than uncover his own darkness. A darkness that, if left to grow in a seedbed of depression, would eventually consume him.

Every holy man that held religion in his heart would chant the same. Hemora's hanging in Refracted Light was a mercy, compared to the blood-draining or poison-induced exorcisms preformed on other fiends of the night.

"You're arguably the worst blood-sucker I've seen. All you do is run from fire and sweat in the presence of blood," Haruka answered, sounding smug.

Using a defeated voice, void of the usual energy, Hemora confessed his first and only sin to the gods.

"It's true. Years back, on my first trip to Valordolt, a young vampiress tricked me, 'gifted' me with this corrupting disease."

Rangar patted his shoulder and Haruka almost bestowed a hug on him – almost. Most would crucify him upon hearing this, but not them, a pair with equal impediments.

Between the pangs for blood and the sleepless nights, it was a raw deal for him. Shape-shifting into a bat sounded amazing at first, but like most of life's benefits, they were nothing compared to the downsides. Now, with a pale, drained mass of flesh under his shell, he was cursed to live as a freak, a monster that scared travellers, fleeing from the mere mention of vampirism.

"Is that why you were imprisoned?" Rangar asked.

"Yep, it's no slew of murders like you two, but.. eh, it's definitely bad," Hemora said, resting on a nearby tree. Turning away, he felt ashamed to even show his undead face. "By the way, thanks for the discretion, Haruka. You could have kept it between us."

"It's not my fault your 'boyfriend' wouldn't move. I'll keep it quiet though, don't worry." Her knack of revealing the truth was uncanny, and Hemora wasn't convinced that she'd keep one of his biggest secrets.

"Tell me one of your secrets. So we're even," he demanded. "Something big, like my vampirism."

"*Sori pec sori sann*, then?" Haruka said.

"Sorry peck sorryson?"

"*Sori pec sori sann*," she repeated slowly. "It's a saying from back home. It roughly means 'secret for secret bond.'"

"Sure whatever that is."

Haruka was reluctant, but eventually decided on one, whether through honourable reasons or simple pity of Hemora's undying life.

"I–I was once a professional dancer," she admitted, also turning away in shame. "*Not* the exotic sort."

For a girl of reform and timid disposition, this was a big deal for her to admit. Hemora loved the idea of her gracefully moving across a stage, making art and not war with her agile talents. The ribbons would spin in motions around her, cutting a vivid halo through a darkened backdrop.

"What? Seriously? That's brilliant, I think that'll do," he said, and laughed at her expense.

"Yes, well, just keep it to yourselves, and I'll keep your little secret under wraps," she said, then looked over to Lucille. "Not even she knows."

Being a fish of the people, Hemora could read faces easier than a child's storybook. However, in her quiet moments, Haruka's look was unchanging and indecipherable. For a youngster, she'd mastered the expression of emptiness, and it made her true feelings hazy, at best.

"You know, it drives me mad. Do you hate Lucille or nah?" Hemora asked.

"To the point. I respect that. I love her spirit, and wish I'd respected it more. But she's a got a conscience, and it'll get her killed. I wish she'd just think of her safety. Killing is bad, but is still a solution when things go south."

Pessimistic as she was, Hemora agreed with her on this point. If only he'd had a darker morality back home, then he'd never have had to leave. Bad as it was, it could've all been avoided with a trident to the heart.

"In my experience, that first push is always the hardest. She'll come around, but –not –alone, aye?"

Nodding, Haruka thanked him for the wise words, then shuffled in closer to the camp. With a slow approach, she sat by Lucille, hopefully to make amends.

Rangar stayed quiet for a time, holding judgement over Hemora, albeit unintentionally. He needed to clear the air and lay some vampiric rumours to rest.

"Don't worry, I'm not a pure-blood, I can't infect any of you. I just get these cravings, you know. I may be a monster, but not by choice." Rangar's judgement disappeared like the illusion it was.

"Fret not, I couldn't shun a man for his affliction. Even if he can be a dick."

Hemora barely believed his words. "You're serious?"

"This is a messy world, full of killers, rapists, and liars. I can forgive a vampire, especially a friend. We're monsters together: the one with ugliness inside, and one on the outside."

It was good to know his secret was out and fairly secure – Hemora had found a true friend, one he could share the feeling of being an outcast with, one who could understand his struggle. The day was nearly over, and he once again prepared for the next big journey to the border with his outcast pal by his side. The first steps were always the hardest, but with company like this, he was finding them slightly less arduous.

Chapter 11: Double-Edged Sword

Kenneth laid down in his bedroll, shut down his senses, and tried to get some sleep. The day was long, and the next, even longer. And being a frail man, he needed his strength.

The quiet of the forest was nice, with no interruptions just like his cell – not that his cell was a good place. One thing shared between his old hell and current heaven was the lack of life – even the cell had an occasional spider. In the distance, Kenneth heard the campfire crackle, and that was it: a warm sound to send him to a warm dream.

"Wakey-wakey," shouted a familiar voice. The ghostly man was walking around the camp trying to grab his attention, and got it, snapping Kenneth from his warmth.

"What do you want?" Kenneth asked, quietly, so as to not attract attention.

The ghost looked at him earnestly. "We need to discuss some things."

"Really? Can it wait till morning? If you can't tell, I've had a long day full of hard work, and I'd love to catch some shut eye," Kenneth replied, with a crankiness to his words.

"And what have you done recently that qualifies as 'hard work'?"

"I lost a couple pints of blood last night. Feeling a little peaky."

What Kenneth had given for Rangar, he'd given it freely. But looking back, he gave a lot, too much for a stranger. Worst of all, because of the brute's disease, the favour could never truly be repaid. No one should ever expect full thanks, but where bloodletting was concerned, a full thanks could be the difference between the warmth of life and the deep ocean of Etheriam.

"You didn't lose blood, you gave it away. An honourable act, but unfortunately, the only one you've managed to make so far," judged the ghost.

"What do you mean?"

"I mean you can't fight for squat. Fumbling at the gates was a pretty shameful display," laughed the spirit.

"Then maybe I'm fit to die by the sword, and nothing else," Kenneth retorted.

"We all start somewhere. I can teach you. *Tomorrow*, of course."

The fisherman just wanted to rest, and would've agreed to anything if it meant he could achieve it. Arguing was an old habit of his, but had been lost to Hart's tortures. With a yawn, he accepted.

"Sure thing, kid. Now can I sleep, Mr..?"

"Greenhill. Xander Greenhill. You may have heard of me," said Xander, posing with hands on hips. "Anyway, nighty-night, Kenneth."

As promptly as he'd arrived, Xander was gone calm as can be, he'd walked out of view, far from the campfire's crackle.

Kenneth regretted asking for a name – now it was a fact that failed to escape his head. The Greenhill family were a famous bunch, all wiped out decades past. The idea of this ghostly aspect being the last remaining member was enough to keep him thinking long into the night.

Xander had ruled the Green Isle, close to the coast, a small world of self-sustained glory. This was until, like most utopian lands, it was reduced to ash, and its legend was morphed into a cautionary tale for the world to hear.

The fall of the Greenhills happened while Kenneth was still a boy, and Xander must've wandered for decades, alone and unheard by everyone besides Krell, a man known for his madness.

If he was the inly sane link between Greenhill and the world, this put the fisherman in a very empowered position. Xander's existence, what little there was of it, remained in his hands.

After pondering Xander's motives and goals long past midnight, Kenneth finally reached his warm dreams; an escape from reality, if only for a few hours.

***

The next day came quickly, and sunlight graced the faces of the Drakeguard in a wave of incandescence. As Harlan made another breakfast, Kenneth practised his swordsmanship with Xander, his ethereal teacher.

It started simply with how to hold Chicardé and taking an appropriate stance for her nimble nature. Light though she was, exhaust caught up with Kenneth quickly. Each stab and every parry felt as though it was knocking the wind right out of him.

Still, he pushed and pushed until his skill manifested, piece by piece. The stabs held less aggression and more precision, and the wind started to catch each speedy swing.

"You're a fast learner, Kenneth, but you still overlook the obvious," Xander chided. "Stand to the side: it gives your opponent less of a target."

"We've been doing this all morning. Can we call it a day?"

"Tired already, old man? You need to be on point for this journey, and every minute you rest dulls that point. Now slide the blade at a more acute angle from your body when you parry."

The Greenhill's weren't known for their swordsmanship – that task fell to their loyal supporters, the Viscount Vass and her score of blade dancers. Kenneth's father had told him stories of Vass, and how the Greenhills were nothing without her. If Xander had no one, that meant he no longer had Vass, and in turn, that meant Kenneth had nothing too.

"Did the Viscount teach you this?" Kenneth questioned. He had grow tired of lectures from a long-dead lord, one who's lacking skill probably caused his death. Xander went quiet for a spell, and it took several minutes of nagging to coax an answer from his purple lips.

"Yes! Okay, yes. She was a wondrous fighter. I… you're lucky to have her teachings here today," Xander sighed. "Now just hold the damn blade to the side."

"I did it like this, back at the gate," he argued, keeping the blade in a horizontal position. "It worked fine then."

"Yes, but that was a single deflection. In the long run you're just wasting stamina that'd be better used on the offensive," Xander countered. The attitude was gruffly thick, familiar even. Again, his father surfaced in Kenneth's memory.

"My pa used to say something like that. *'Ya think too short-term, Kenny. Planning catches perfection. Pride only hooks pettiness'*, or something of the sort," he replied, vocalising a gravelled imitation of his father.

Papa Porter hadn't crossed his mind for an age. His dad's place in his life had been thankfully small, and as such, Kenneth spent a short, yet pleasant amount of time remembering him.

Looking back, it was easy to see history repeating itself on a small scale: Kenneth treated his family the same as his papa treated him – distantly. Maybe that's why he'd lost them? Just like pa.

Xander looked pensive. "Your father was right you know. The whole reason I'm stuck in my compromising form is because of planning."

"What kind: poor or perfect?" Kenneth asked.

"Does it matter? I've been thrown out of my own body because of my choices, and now my mission is to find a way forward. I need to move on."

"You don't want to go back to it? A body does have its perks," the fisherman recommended, firmly pounding his chest.

"I think it's too late to go back now. The only place I can go from here is paradise," Xander replied, with woeful confidence. The ghost looked down at his stigmatised hands and sighed. "Besides, I'm fond of not feeling the pain any more. Leave that to some other schmuck."

A depressing result regardless: living alone or dying. Kenneth truly felt for his mentor in that moment. If Philip hadn't whisked him away from his chains, a similar fate would've dominated him.

"What happened when you became a spirit?"

"Honestly, I can't recall. A combination of time and trauma has robbed me of my former memories."

Kenneth scoffed. "Typical. Guys like us can't catch a break."

As if a torch had been snuffed, Xander retracted into his shell, and put some distance between them, severing contact to the only sane bridge that connected him to Magnus. No one – man nor elf – should be subject to loneliness; Kenneth knew this all too well. Moving over with Chicardé in hand, he made a half-cocked attempt to console the ghost with his presence.

Xander ignored the pause and replied to him as though it never happened. "Isn't that the truth. I think we're done now, Kenneth. Best head back to camp and grab some grub before Harlan eats it all."

The fisherman couldn't argue against filling his belly, and swung back around and head back to camp. His carefree swing caused Chicardé to fly from his grip and nearly grazed the melancholy ghost. He was surprised to see Xander recoil in fear and nearly jump out of his metaphorical skin.

Dodging out of Chicardé's path, the ghostly elf screamed, "Careful with that!" He'd instilled such a cower in his voice that his purple glow almost became a sickly shade of yellow.

"What's wrong? You're see-through, kid." Kenneth reassured him, punching his empty hand right through Xander's shaking body.

"No, NO! You don't know! Chicardé is more than that: illethium's more than that." On the verge of crying though his scared eyes, Xander lost his breath, only to regain it and his composure soon after. "That metal is something most gods fear. It can cut *anything*. All flesh, whether meaty, magic, or holy, will all tear at its edge. My form's *only* magic, and she'll pop me like a pimple."

Still new to ghostly custom, not even knowing the magic behind it, Kenneth dropped the sword's tip to face the ground. This wiped all anguish from his mentor's words, and earned him a quiet "Thanks."

"Ahoy-hoy, Mr. Porter," called a cheery Hericore, marching through the mounds of grass and pillars of wood. "How are we doing this fine morn?"

"I'm... good, sir, just practising." Keeping his ghostly friend a secret, Kenneth jumped around for a time, showing off some swings and stabs.

"Ah, Heri. A kind visit, but what could he be yearning for?" Xander pondered, casting doubt on the situation. "Surely he didn't come out here to check up on you? Maybe he's here to talk about your spa treatment in Central?"

"We moving out?" Kenneth asked, simplifying Xander's logical leaps.

"Actually, no… I… I just wanted to talk about your time in Hart's 'care,' and what he did–"

The drake was hitting a touchy subject, Kenneth feigned tiredness and begged for a rescheduled trip down memory lane. After travelling too far down that road with Xander, he wasn't willing to make a second trip with another, especially a corporeal other. In the last day, he'd taken a liking to the secrecy involved with the ghost.

"Of course. The perils of looking back can often be tiresome in of themselves. Perhaps another time?" Hericore suggested, looking straight through the fisherman with a suggestive stare, his meaning hard to decipher. "I've saved you some breakfast, Kenneth. Your imprisonment might be a secret, but your waistline is not. You're absolutely famished."

Agreeing, the fisherman sheathed Chicardé and returned to camp. Grabbing a bowl of famous Ainsworth stew, he readied himself for the trip further south.

Xander kept in close proximity to him, but hesitated to approach Chicardé again, and the hand that carried her. A hand that held the power to kill without limits was a scary one indeed.

***

The sun's glow soon surrendered to the dark clouds, allowing the dullness of mid-spring to return. Ever-driven, the Drakeguard pushed on to Lake Vita.

A fishing village once circled the lake, back when it still had fish to inhabit it, before dying with the rest of the animals in Vita. Kenneth would've loved to spend a week or two there, fishing his problems away, but was robbed of this opportunity by the Order – half his life had been stolen by the Order. But one thing the Order couldn't tarnish was the sheer size of the lake, which spanned a half mile in length and reflected the travellers as they passed its shallow shore.

"It's like any other pool," Hemora dismissed.

"Not at all," Kenneth challenged. "It's got a green tint to it. A bunch of algae still grows on its bed."

"Should tell that to the Order. *'Hey fellas, you missed a spot'*. It'd be priceless."

"You laugh, but letting it grow too long is unhealthy. The surrounding plants will start to suffer," Kenneth preached.

"That's all life is. One group falls, another grows too large and is next to face the axe," Haruka butted in, sulking at the back of the group. "*Roudunta viteiru*: the circle of life."

She and Lucille still remained separated, opposites too distant to attract each other. It was a saddening sight. Though their distance was slowly closing, the idea of it existing in the first place spoke ill of the pair's ideals. A good argument either brought people together or tore them apart; a bad argument could fluctuate any rapport.

Hericore stopped everyone, as he'd done the day before, in order to lay down the camp boundaries. This time, they were placed in a grove, out of view of the lake. The trees surrounding them were thin, but densely placed. This grove was one of few.

"This will be the last chance you'll have to bathe until Karin, and possibly even Barsameil. Make use of the lake and all it has to offer. It's nature's gift to you and I."

"Best news all day. I could use some time to relax and refresh," Lucille smiled.

"Age before beauty," Harlan claimed, practically pushing past her.

"Hold on, ladies first." Demanding and commanding, she stopped him from moving to the lake's edge. All it took was a thin arm and a determined voice to halt the dwarf of legends.

In a playful manner, Harlan met her demands, only to deny them.

"And you'd stop me?"

"Hell yes, I would. I haven't seen clean water in nearly a week."

"A week? Try three months," moaned Hemora. "Hanging cells have no time for hygiene."

"You were a hanged man? How on Magnus did you earn a place there?" Lucille raised a good question – a select few make it to such a deplorable living state in Refracted Light.

"You know... *bad stuff.*"

"Bad stuff?" she repeated, with a raised eyebrow.

Hemora tutted. "Yeah. Now let us lads pass."

"Fine. Just keep your flesh trident away from me, and we're golden."

Travis led the men into the murky waters of the lake. Hemora, being a child of the ocean, loved to jump right into the deepest corners of the green-tinted depths, and pulled away from everyone else. Harlan had an opposing philosophy. Being a master of fire and heat, he refrained from getting more than waist-deep in the algae-less pools, staying on one of the rocky shore. Kenneth remained with the others and stripped down to his skivvies.

It hadn't dawned on him until then, what a mess Hart had left him in. Years of inactivity had turned healthy, muscular legs into thin poles of grey hair atop two crooked feet. The ribcage he owned was showing in its full, and could be played like an instrument; he felt so hollow inside.

Compared to Rangar's bursting pectorals or even Harlan's rolls of fat, Kenneth lacked mass to call his own. The worst of all was his heart. It physically felt so weak and shrivelled over the years that even standing still was a challenge now.

None of the others cared to mention his declining looks. Maybe it didn't need a comment? He was a dying man, far past any sort of prime, and this trip south could be his last.

They bathed naked, with the exception of Harlan, who decided against revealing his personal side, unlike Rangar. The scales were odd, but apart from them he looked ripped, from pecs to abs – all toned – down to an unwieldy member, another part unfortunately still gripped by scales.

Comparing sizes was an art form to some men, but to many others – Kenneth included – putting a ruler to the flesh was an uncomfortable action, fitting for men of a different persuasion. His father had made sure to beat a few rules into him at a young age, and made sure sexual ignorance was one of them.

Now free from the shackles of abuse, both parental and criminal, it seemed fair to break such an aged rule. But, wading through a past of canings, lashings, and slaps was a difficult thing. Leaving dad's swamp of mind-bogging views wouldn't come easily.

"So Travis, how did a person like yourself meet with a... character, like Helena?" asked Hemora.

"Me and her started a band of adventurers back in the day; called ourselves the Vagabonds. Creative, I know, but we had some fun times," the cleric reminisced.

"Fun?" Rangar questioned.

"It was terrifying. Everything we did led to the worst Magnus had to offer: giants, dragons, goblins. But between the horrors, we truly had a good laugh."

Camaraderie of that magnitude was uncommon amongst the older generation, and Kenneth never indulged in joining a team of... anything, really. From lone fisherman, to lone criminal, to lone Drakeguard, he gave the same welcome that he received from others. Over time, this had made him a single soul, finding partnership in only the romantic sense.

"Helena's great, but would you screw her?" asked Hemora, bluntly corrupting the talk.

"*No!*" replied Travis, as his voice cracked under the vulgarity of the question. "*Why*? Why would you ask me that?"

"Just wondering. Hey, Harlan! Would you screw Helena?!"

"I don't know. She's sporting a nice pair, but she's also a little too close to her bird," the dwarf replied with a foolish hesitation.

Kenneth could almost see the cogs whirring in Hemora's perverse mind. "I could imagine she lets it watch, you know. Some type of reverse bestiality. Freaky shit."

The molluskan painted a vivid picture as he thrusted his pelvis on the spot while projecting a mockery of Bella's cawing. Immature, but amusing. Kenneth had lost plenty to age, but a childish sense of humour still lived on.

"Bestiality? You're a fish!" Travis said, defending Helena's already iron will. Hemora then ceased his thrusts and escalated the increasingly disturbing chatter.

"Now that. That's just racist," the molluskan mockingly accused.

Travis recoiled. "What? No. I'm not a racist. I'm not."

"That's exactly what a racist would say," Rangar said, posing a strong point. Under the pressuring scrutiny, Travis began to sweat.

"I'd... I'd never judge another–"

"It's cool. I'm pulling your leg, Travis. I couldn't give a rat's ass if you were or not," Hemora said. "No slime off my shell."

"Oh boy, that's a relief... The joking part, not the racism part. I'm no purveyor of hatred."

The air had an awkward thickness to it, something Travis carried with him, but Rangar sought to break the silence that rose from the butchered talk.

"Fair play, Travis. What about you, old man? Was this mangy mutt once a hound dog?" asked Rangar.

"Who, me?" He and Harlan answered together, proving age wasn't just an external feeling.

Rangar paused. "Err... the actual old looking one, I guess."

"Don't know, don't care," Kenneth replied. "Stay stuck in a room for twenty years, and you tend to lose your lust for pretty much everything that exists outside said room." The memories of the solitary existence flooded back, and slicked his mind in sorrow.

Helena was an attractive woman, but didn't hold a candle to his wife, Kaitlyn. She was the whole deal: personality, looks, and smarts; maybe too smart.

"Barring the bird, you'd plough her though, right Harlan?" Hemora said.

Harlan sighed longingly. "Sorry kids, my heart is set on another. Someone with the sweet scent of flowers in her hair."

"Give up the nice talk. We all know it's Lucille you're rambling about," Rangar chuckled.

"Really? That obvious?"

"Definitely," Kenneth added.

"Even I knew," Travis said.

"Well, so much for the secret admirer gimmick. Any idea how to break it to her?" Harlan asked, unintentionally avoiding Travis' input.

Not having any experience other than his first attempt at courtship, Kenneth only offered a little, but it meant so much more to him.

"I think flowers are a good idea. I picked them for my wife when we first met."

"Yeah, but that's a little niche. It's been half a century since people did that crap," said Hemora.

"Half a century? Fifty years? I wasn't a toddler when I married my wife."

"They did like to marry young back then," said Rangar, having a warped insight.

It had been Kenneth's fifteenth year when he'd met Kaitlyn, a fisherman's child like him. At sixteen they were married, and seventeen bore a child, with another at eighteen and nineteen. Each year gave another miscarriage, until a miracle came from stillborn blood, and darling Rosalyn came to life. Kenneth had grown up too fast, and spent the later years ruminating on his flawed choices in life. Kate hadn't been one of them.

"I'm more shocked you have a wife," Hemora said.

"What, you think Hart's scorn stole all my life from me? I saved some room for the scorn of marriage," Kenneth joked.

"Hart actually has a reason to hate you? I just assumed he was a dick, and I left the rumours at the door."

The molluskan loved to assume. Assumptions were plagues, each and every one. It was the same plague that rotted Kenneth's title and credence. It was the reason he lived in the Ripper's shadow, much like Harlan bore the mantle of 'Short Fuse.'

"It's never that simple. He had a reason," Rangar said, implying guilt on Kenneth's part. The fisherman didn't answer and remained silent. It was better this way, and the past would remain buried – for now.

Everything turned to quiet again; Hemora dropped the question, and Rangar picked up the pieces.

"Sooo..." Rangar paused. "Harlan, what about you? How did you end up in that gaping maw of a prison?"

Harlan, being much more forward than Kenneth, gave up his tale of arrest; spun with truthful words, a claim he was unsure anyone could match.

"Hitch up, lads, and cast your minds back thirty years to the Depressive Wail of the Fifth Era," Harlan grandly began.

"I wasn't alive then," Travis said, followed by Hemora's same confession.

"I was only a babe," Rangar also admitted.

"Well then, Ken, cast your mind back, and the rest of you children can learn a thing or two from this," Harlan continued, discontented with old age.

Taking in the warming waters of Vita, Kenneth did as Harlan said, and travelled back to Fifth's End. Following the civil disputes in the west, several of Midgartt's leaders could barely find two roths to rub together back then.

The Order, Caster's Council, and the Helmlord all gave too much in a war that wasn't theirs to fight. Thousands died, more bled, and in the aftermath, only the labourers survived.

He and the fisherman of Betiel were such survivors, making a fine living on a booming fish market, forgoing even family in the pursuit of a safe future. But to those who could find a stable business, only hardship awaited. Bread was the standard meal, all day, every day.

Houses? Forget houses. The fields and valleys were home to most men, not stone shacks. Looking back, it was a time warmer than Vita for Kenneth, but built on the backs of suffering swordsman and smiths. The depression drained the very soul from people, but the Deep never drained anything from him, and he loved her for it.

With poor hand puppetry, Harlan continued his tale. "I had a pretty tough time in the ruins of Valordolt. Because they were just that – ruins. All the carpenters died in the wars. I'd lost my own job and my thirteenth pet dog."

"You lost a dog? Did it run away?" Travis said, confused.

"Well. I ate my thirteen dog," Harlan confessed, pulling a face of realised horror. Hastily continuing, he asked, "Anyway, you know those bulbous bottles of blue beer, with the little pieces of silver floating inside?" The younger men shook their heads.

"I do," Kenneth said. "Teal of Tealka, an old drink from molluskan waters."

Never a supporter of drinks with queer motives, Kenneth had never allowed a Teal of Tealka to grace his lips, among other things. In the broken economy of Fifth's End, all his wealth would have vanished after just one bottle of the luxury drink.

"So after losing my source of income, I understandably lost control, and things began to heat up," Harlan regretted, sounding more unsure with each passing sentence. "Long story short: I went on a bit of a bender, drank a crate of those Teal beauties, and accidentally burned down a chapel."

"Damn. How did the Order not cut you down right then and there?" said Hemora, in amazement of the drunken feat.

"Turns out Hart has a soft spot for me. I introduced him to an old friend of mine, and he saved my ass from the chopping block."

"Hart can show mercy? Who knew," Kenneth said, as he dragged his withered hide from the waters and began drying off.

He felt jealous of Harlan's granted mercy. He'd been fed to the wolves a thousand times over for a miscarriage of justice, and Ainsworth got a few years inside for a full scale offence.

Jealousy was new to him, and it quickly faded. Hart was the cause, nothing Harlan could've done would've stopped the abuse; the gods treated all their creations unequally, and mortal men were the same. Only the gods had the good grace to let it all end eventually. Hart did not.

Chapter 12: Downpour

Lucille listened for the men's return, and when they finally dragged their soggy asses back to camp, she was led to the lake, alongside Haruka and Helena.

Lake Vita sat still, once containing over a hundred breeds of fish and aquatic insects. Now it rested, hollow and lifeless; an ironic circumstance given its name. Though empty, the lake was comforting, topping any hot spring Lucille had travelled to back home. The heat reminded her of Harlan, as it covered her, relaxing the muscles and tingling several areas sensitive to her.

She was first to dive into the lonely waters, craving a relaxing dip like this for months now. Haruka held a more steady approach, and Helena waited for her hawk to enter waters before she did. They all stripped down, aside from Helena – who kept her undergarments – then unwound, something even the world's end could wait for.

After dozens of stone cold showers in Refracted Light, Lucille had seen Haruka's petite body before. The pale girl had a strange beauty in her small frame – everything held a nice shape, from perky breasts to jimp hips and all that rested between. Haruka had always held a spot on Lucille's 'to do list', if only they'd shared the same appetites.

Helena was far different. Her body had more excess fat, but also gave a more comforting appearance than the sharpness of Haruka. Without drawing too much attention with her gazing, Lucille cleared a space on her list for the gunslinger, taking a firm liking to her firm rear. Helena may have to compensate with make-up, but everything else was all natural, and Lucille loved it. Appreciation at its finest…. This was until the Karinese cutie turn back from her, and revealed a tragic past.

Helena was coated from nape to hips in deep scars caused by even deeper cuts. It was disturbing to see so many white scars stretched across her brown back, almost warranting a tear of appreciation; not for Helena's pain, but for her bravery. Marks so clear must have been old – a decade so, at least. This meant the bold woman was just a bold girl when they were afflicted. The 'how' and 'who' weren't needed to paint the vivid picture of their origin, and Lucille didn't linger on their cause for long.

Even when she bathed, Helena was persistent, wearing her mask and hat at all times. Keeping her face above the water was probably for the best; while on the run from the law, make up wouldn't be easy to come by. After witnessing the damage across her back, Lucille's mind wandered, imagining what could linger under her pampered facade. Even with scars and all, the gunslinger was a beauty. It was a tragedy of its own that Lucille didn't look as good in comparison. Lucille always kept fit, but physical fitness didn't always match physical finesse.

Perverse observations aside, Lucille got to work scrubbing up and down her body, leaving no inch of flesh unclean, quite literally washing away her problems. Helena followed the thorough method, but took breaks to also remove the dirt from Bella's talons.

"You wash with your beast?" Haruka noted disapprovingly.

"She's no beast. Birds are just like us; they need their releases too," said Helena as she ran her fingers through Bella's sable feathers.

"What happened to your bat?" asked Lucille, missing the little puffball. "It saved my bacon, then disappeared."

Helena answered with an odd stare.

"I don't have a bat. I've hated the pests ever since Fort Palmer. Those flappy demons know better than to approach me."

In an equal state of discord, Lucille replied, "But a bat delivered a message on your behalf; it's how we returned to the gate in one piece."

"I never wrote a message. I can barely write."

"Well, it's best we don't look too far into it," dissuaded Haruka. "It isn't the strangest thing to happen recently. That honour lies with St. Belmont's going boom."

Haruka was a sleepless wreck under the thumb of paranoia, and left no rock unturned in efforts to quench suspicion. Now, she had no fears of the unknown, and this in itself was an unknown fear. First reckless violence, now fleeting fear. What was Haruka becoming?

"I trust Hericore is telling the truth: we had no ill will regarding that clock tower," interrupted Helena, "I'd say the strangest thing is Lu getting real friendly with Harlan."

At the mention of his name, Lucille's gaunt cheeks went rose red, giving the appearance of two ripe apples. It wasn't the first time this had happened, and this one was as uncontrollable as the last.

"Oh, it's not like that. Harlan's a really funny, honest guy. Not many of them around anymore"

"You and me might differ on the use of the word 'funny'," Helena disregarded, "and of course there's no one like him: his ilk died two eras past."

"Well I *like* him, and that's all," Lucille repressed. "He's like a big pussycat."

"He may be, but you're still a little chick. I'd steer clear of that mess of a man, lest we forget the incident with Donsis." The mood took a dive with the return of Donsis' hateful presence. Like a plague, it lingered in their hearts still. It didn't linger for long, and Helena's questions found a new mark. "What about you, killer? Any of the fellas grab your eye?"

Haruka stared with unhappiness at the thought. Maybe she wasn't truly free of fear?

"We're waging an impossible war against an incredibly wealthy, powerful tyrant, and you're interested in who I'm attracted to?" she replied slowly.

Helena smiled with a nod. "Yes, yes I am, darling."

"None of them interest me. I barely know them, and I've little time for romance."

"Geez, killer, I wasn't talking 'bout romance. Okay then, personality aside, which one has the best body?" the gunslinger pressed.

Lucille never really thought of what could lie under the guys' armour; between the bloody murder and fires, she lost attention in that department. The muscles of a man's abs were no different from the fat in her chest: a wonderful distraction from the heart that lies beneath.

"If it keeps you two quiet. I guess... I like the look of Travis more than the others," Haruka replied.

"Really, Travis? The only man I know that suits a dress?" Helena said, holding off unwanted laughter.

Haruka's eyes flared up, and what would've been a moment of friendly construction turned to destruction in an instant. "Sorry, darling," Helena backtracked, "But he's the only guy I know weedier than my squeeze, and Philip's no beefcake, that's for sure."

"How did you end up with Philip, anyway? He seems like a big narcissistic jerk to me. No offence," Lucille wondered. In the minutes she'd been witness to Philip, he'd not left the best of impressions.

"None taken. Philip can be a little... arrogant sometimes. But he's a sweetheart on the inside. I remember when we first met, he told me I was as beautiful as Valentine and twice as lovely. I didn't think much of him at the time – he was a shy fella. Then one day, he just *transformed* into this man of pure confidence and command. That's the man I'm smitten with," swooned Helena, with heart on her naked sleeve.

"Sounds romantic," said Haruka. "Or desperate," she added, under her breath.

After purging the blood and ashes from herself, Lucille left the lake's company before the others, hoping to find a moment of solace in the forest. Vita was relaxing, but this was the real refreshing part; internal closure.

Wrapped in her prison rags, which she'd re-purposed into baggy underwear and an itchy brassiere, she planted herself on an oak stump, let go of the ill tidings she held, and began to reset her very feelings. Under the rainy sky she focused inwards, and put her worries to rest. Forgiveness was her weapon, and using it on Haruka was the only option left.

This didn't last long, however, as Harlan came stumbling into view, head to the ground. Holding a handful of pale, purple flowers – likely daphnes – it was equally rude as it was odd.

Rising from her seat, covering herself in what little foliage was available, Lucille addressed the wandering dwarf.

"Harlan! What in Beth's glorious name are you doing?" she said, startling him and grabbing his undivided attention.

"L... Lucille, what are... I... I? Put a shirt on. *Please*," Harlan fumbled, shielding his face from her exposed body. It was nice to be host to a male audience, and one that actually cared for her decency, a rare gift. Deep down, she didn't care if he looked or not.

"Compose yourself, Harlan. I bet you've seen a women's body hundreds of times in your day," she said softly to calm the dwarf. "I'm nothing special."

"That's not true. You're plenty special." With some encouragement, his hands lowered and the dumbfounded dwarf regained his thoughts. "I didn't mean to see... whatever *this* is."

"No, you didn't. You're just picking flowers?"

"Right, I am," he paused. "Hericore wants them... for dinner. Berries for dinner. Yes, berries to spice it up."

"We're eating daphne berries? Aren't those poisonous?"

Harlan paused, then pasted on an uneasy smile. "Midgartt's Greatest Chef, three centuries running. I can turn poisons to perfection." He was hiding something, but she never had the chance to pursue it, as mother nature intervened.

A freak flash storm smacked the face of Magnus, like no other before it. Its waters swept both of them to the ground, quickly muddying the earth beneath them. These kind of spring rainfalls only lasted a few minutes, but dropped rivers of water in their short spans, flooding any caught in their weeping gales.

When the flood's worst was over, Lucille pulled herself up, now covered in a dark layer of mud all over, totally nullifying her extended time in the lake. Harlan was also coated, but instead of being angry, he laughed at the misfortune, and even more so when he saw her wasted rest.

"Not quite the mud baths you're used to?" he mocked, cleaning her eyes of muck.

Harlan was idiotic and full of puns, but she loved his optimism. With a newly formed puddle at her feet, she had a bout of idiocy to match.

"A real hothead, ain't cha? Think you need to cool off."

Using her left foot, she flicked the water at Harlan's large head. Her accuracy was impeccable, and drowned the dwarf, knocking him back to the muddy earth.

His response? To return fire. This started a long water fight that lasted throughout the remainder of the storm. It was stupid, it was childish, but also one hell of a fun time, and one that cleared her head more than any internal reflection would've done.

When the rain slowed to a spit, and the setting sun finally broke through the clouds, the picture created by the two transcended mere awe and wonder. Finding a memory to replace the muddy pair staring at the warm sun, letting it heat their chilled bodies, with their feet submerged in the cool waters would be a hard task.

This was paradise to Lucille, not too hot or cold, surrounded by homely forests, and accompanied by a like-minded soul. Grabbing what remained of the washed away daphnes, she saw right through Harlan's ruse. Handing the single flower back, she cheekily said, "Keep trying, chef. I'm sure you'll get there soon."

Though his advances were washed away by fate, Lucille still appreciated the gesture, and felt a twinge of something more deep down. A single butterfly fluttered in her stomach, awaiting company.

Chapter 13: Rebirth

Ash mulled over those words – *'the gift has arrived'* – as though it meant something to him. Little did he know, these words meant everything to him. For the second time in his life, he was denied death, only this time it was involuntary, extending the reign of the thankless hero.

With a bad taste of phlegm in his mouth, and a swirling unbalance of equilibrium, it felt like he'd woken up from a bad dream, but his aches and pains were very real. He had expected to awake in the afterlife as an immortal soul birthed anew, free to swim for eternity. This wasn't the case.

Along with the physical trauma from the fight – all throbs and stabs – he also heard a stream of static in his head, which ping-ponged throughout his skull without heed.

"Ugh, where am I?" Ash said to himself.

Though no one was in the room, he felt accompanied, and the words felt as though he spoke to someone preoccupied, unable to answer despite their proximity. To make things worse, his throat was hoarse, and the gravelly voice he owned was alternating between his regular accent and one of a high-born descent, holding the weathered chimes of an older gentleman.

The cracked armour he wore was missing, and only shorts covered an equally cracked body. Sitting up on the gurney that he rested on, Ash inspected the dark room that clearly wasn't were he'd collapsed.

It was small enough to house one person, and was devoid of windows, aside from a rectangular slot, far above the gurney. The walls were eroding, with sunlight shining though the holes in the mortar. Disrepair gripped most places these days, presenting no indication of Ash's whereabouts.

A smell of rotting meat hung in the air, and the large visible stitching across his stomach suggested a recent surgery; a disheartening thought, considering the deplorable condition of the room. His hairy body was carved in the strangest of fashions. Each scar had a different pattern, and each pain felt just as varied.

Never the bed-bound sort, he pressed on. "Well, let's get moving. This gut ain't gonna fill itself."

Around the room sat jars of what could only be described as biological trash. Some held lumps of discoloured flesh, with no distinguishable origin, while others contained bisected organs and members of all sorts. One container even held part of a crystivine.

Floating in a viscous gel, the pink crystal mumbled prayers even after being dissected from the host. All life had a field of arcana around it; it was what granted them with the quality of being 'alive.' Since angels had so much arcane power, even their severed parts gained sentience. Ash wondered if Zarpadon had ever lost a part of himself and accidentally 'fathered' a lil' Zarp.

The jars looked and felt wrong, but the worst of them was a stubby, diced ear that looked identical to his own left ear. It couldn't have been his – he could hear without flaw, and most definitely still owned two ears.

Putting the worry to rest, the dwarf rubbed the side of his dome where the ear should be. Running his fingers up a long triangular ear to a pointed tip, Ash's heart sank. It was an elf's ear, grafted in the old one's place.

Along with the shock came a wave of nausea, as the static turned to a high-pitched scratching sound that deafened him from the inside. Something deep was breaking free, and he couldn't withhold its escape.

He felt strange. Bravery up and left him, and everything about the situation scared the mighty dwarf; odd, given his hardy past. Then came the feeling of ownership, almost as if the world itself owed him a great debt. Greed like this was another foreign emotion, and shadows danced around him, ready to attack.

Ash opened the door out into the rest of the building, attempting to run from the hostile shades. But then his mind tore in two, his legs gave, and he dropped to his knees, clutching his quivering skull in pain.

Lying in agony, he spied a reflection of his broken visage in a mirror. This rounded relic was mostly covered by cloth, left to gather dust in this ramshackle place. Through a tear in the fabric, he saw himself, and it wasn't pretty.

A thin, toothy jaw replaced his old one; all gum, no muscle. The sideburns he wore with former pride were separated, with the left one vanished, and in its place rested only a smooth streak of almond-skinned jawline. The ear and the jaw matched, connected to him with little grace; even now, the stitches were thick and tight.

"What's happened to me?" Ash muttered feverishly, fading out of consciousness.

Once more, the static noise rung around his head and slowly turned to unintelligible whispers calling out to him. It all ended with a thankful, foreign call from within.

"I'm... alive?"

***

The next time Ash awoke, a figure watched from the shadows which had calmed from earlier.

"Wake up, warrior. Maybe at snail's pace, this time," said the croaky woman.

"What happened? My head... Where? Hart, please, we can talk?" he mumbled, speaking in broken sentences that weren't his.

"Take it easy, warrior. Your minds are trying to exist in tandem, trying to merge recent memories together," she warned. "In time, all will pass. Then you can introduce yourselves."

Ash concentrated on the voice in his head, which now returned to static mumbles and screams of terror. Eventually the headaches weakened, and his mind became clear once more.

"What happened? I died, I –I felt it."

"Indeed, you did. I saved you – both of you."

"Saved me? Saved us? Us? We..." The static lingered on.

"Brace yourself, warrior. The knowledge I'm about to bestow upon you is most troubling," the woman sighed. "Yes, I saved you, but the only way I could was by binding your body, mind and soul with another. Don't let it–"

"Wait, you bound me? Like –like a thrall?! Are you some sort of necromancer?!" Ash gasped in dread.

Necromancers were not the most socially accepted folks on Magnus, with their practises heavily discouraged. It was one thing for the church to save the living, but saving the dead was another matter completely.

The Order had fought the purloiners of rot for so long that both factions were tied in the annals of time, life and death in an ever-lasting war for dominance. As such, Ash had spent his career putting necrotic slavers to the axe. He wasn't allowing the very crones he spat on to save him now.

"Please don't use that word. I am – by definition – a necromancer. However, I believe the definition is a tad overdue for some revisions. My methods are unorthodox, foreign to any other necrotic school on Magnus."

"I see no difference," Ash said, full of spite, looking over his scared and pale corpse of a body. "I died, and now I'm back against my will. Necromancy through and through."

"You know so very little of how I operate, so I'd keep those opinions to yourself. Besides, if I wasn't a 'necromancer', then you'd both be dead," said the figure, stepping out of the shadows to reveal herself.

Ash stared at the old, hunched woman, with her withered hands and tightly-pulled yet withered skin. Her nose was wart-ridden, and her face was thin. Covered with several layers of purple robes and held together by ropes and frayed knots, the woman showed age, great age, yet her eyes shone with a youthful glow, making her appear unnatural in the dim light. "I'm Madame Osiris, and I run this slice of holy ground," she claimed, stomping at the planks beneath them.

Holy ground would be a stretch for this run-down dump. It appeared to closely resemble a drug den, not a place of worship. 'Holy mixed with horrid' was a fitting term for the tenement and Osiris herself. Though haggish, her voice was... strange. Off-putting was a better term, as it didn't quite match her age.

"The pleasure's all mine," Ash scoffed with a noticeable lack of enthusiasm. "The name's Ash Belwert. Paladin under the orders of Hericore, the Red Drake."

This introduction could all be lies now. With an undetermined amount of time passing between leaving Valordolt and now, Hericore's journey could've come and gone.

Osiris handed him a purple vial of lumpy liquid that had a rotten smell so powerful it breached the glass tube it lived in.

"You should drink. It helps alleviate the pains of the past."

"So it's like alcohol?"

"Of sorts. It is a family recipe. A closely kept drink that binds this cult I rule."

"Cult?" Ash gritted, feeling even more unhappy about his current company and her shrouded intent. Those that handled their cults well could rebrand and take the moniker of 'religion'. The Order followed this path once, back in their early years.

"My Cult of the Unity is a testament to the gods of death and undeath alike. In addition, it acts in defiance of the Order's fake notions of purity."

Ash paused and placed his head in hands. Necromancy was the magic of undeath, unlike arcane magic, which acted as the force of life. When the body died and was preserved from rot, its arcane force stagnated into a cold and weighty source of energy. Where a living soul was bound by lightly arcane power, an undead was lumbering and ghastly; living while dead, on Magnus when they shouldn't be.

Masters of the macabre necrotic arts could enslave the soul before it was taken to heaven, and in essence 'own' their undead projects. Ash didn't feel enslaved, but did have a weight to him that hadn't been there prior to the battle. Coupled with an ever-present dizziness, all signs pointed to his undying fate.

"So I'm an undead abomination. *Damn it*. Damn it all to hell."

"An abomination? Not at all. As I've said, I differ from others of my ilk. My methods don't allow death, only rebirth," Osiris prompted, lowering her robes to show a scar cut across her neck, "I am also patchwork, bound to breed more salvation, like you and your patched partner."

Her words did little to ease Ash's dislike. Dabblers in death were all the same – some worshipped Lilith, some Aldrich, but all worked against Bethany to taint the order of Magnus. Now Ash contributed to this pool of degenerates.

"Charming, I'm not alone in my abuse of life. Who is it that I'm bound with? Another chump of vitality, like me?" the dwarf wondered.

"I know not the name, but he was an elf from the holy city," admitted Osiris. "Drink. The brew will pave the way to the name you seek."

Weighing his wonderment against common sense, Ash chose to neck the purple goo down his throat quickly, so as to avoid the taste. Time seemed to slow as a voice, distorted at first, slowly appeared, then migrated further away. Shortly, his body was completely taken.

"Arrgghh... Life. How I missed you so," said a horribly recognisable voice. It came from Ash's mouth and energetically moved his body around, but wasn't him. This snivelling voice was that of Donsis Allisteel.

"Welcome back, passenger. Do you find this body suitable?" greeted Osiris.

"Everything feels... heavy. Heavy yet small at the same time. But that's cave dwellers for you, I suppose," the elf complained.

Ash wouldn't stand for this. It was his body, and he took it back from the greedy claws of Donsis.

"Get out of my head," he snarled. But Donsis refused.

"No way," Donsis said, childishly clambering around their shared brain. It held no pain, but did feel vile, as if the elf had sneaked a peek at his most intimate moments. The violation had to end.

"You despise dwarves."

"Yes, but when my options are death or dweller, I make do," Donsis reasoned.

"The two of you already know each other?" Osiris asked.

Ash tried to hold control, but with a weakened grip he faltered, and everything started to fuzz at the edges; he was losing reality by the second.

"Donsis? No, no, this can't be. I'm not... Donsis, I'm Ash–sis. I'm, Adon–sh. I'm Adonis. Adonis?" The two struggled to cope. Ash continued denying rebirth while Donsis denied death.

"Adonis? Good, it seems your personalities have created a new name for yourself. It will become easier with time. Trust me," congratulated Osiris.

"Adonis. No that's a stupid name," Ash denied.

"Keep drinking. Purity through constriction is the only truth you need, and truth will out." She smiled with a wise gaze, showing she'd had this talk before. "It'll get worst before better: in both taste and effect. Aside from helping with the process, you'll soon be able to divide up control more diplomatically. You should be able to walk without passing out. Come! To the kitchens. My boys have a bowl of porridge waiting." Being a woman of great presence, Osiris left the paired minds together, and emptiness ensued.

Ash wanted only to rest, but the second half, his lesser half, was caught in panic.

"I can't be dead. I can't be melded with a filthy dwarf!"

"This is no easy job for me either, pal. I can't believe this. I was ready to die in that field. No rest for the wicked, aye," Ash assuredly said.

"I need a mirror, and I need porridge." And just like that, they worked up the strength to exit the room, facing the long day ahead.

Soon enough, breakfast became the centre of Ash's attention. It was nice to see some things hadn't changed. He ate a sweet, but thick, bowl of porridge, washing it down with another purple bottle. Osiris recommend only six doses a day, but he never was good with portion control, as evidenced by his large frame of bone and muscle.

The drink was a potion she named 'Bluvon Opi', whatever that meant; most likely some outlandish tongue that translated poorly into the global lingua franca. Each sip of Bluvon Opi pushed Donsis back into the deep labyrinth of Ash's mind, but also weakened his own dominance to a type of internal stalemate. Neither was their master of the body, and it was for the best.

The Cult's kitchen was like the rest of the building, and the rotting wood of the furniture matched the equally rotten jars of flesh that surrounded the uncomfortable chairs. A few burners of incense littered the room, making a feeble attempt to best the rotten smells. It only managed to besmirch the smell lavender in Ash's mind. He didn't care, though. The resurrection process caused quite a hunger, and even the questionable bowl of porridge was enough to satiate his pangs.

"I hate porridge," Donsis moaned.

"Best breakfast around. You best get used to the taste," Ash replied.

"You seem to have two minds on everything," said Osiris, "one of many possible side effects from your revival. You may also experience unwanted feelings during certain events, echoes of your past personalities creeping in on each other, a dance that is more glorious than terrifying."

Their return to the land of the living was accompanied by a great negativity. Ash continued to wish this all a dream. Rubbing his brow, a faint sigh followed.

"I know, I can already feel a change. There's this underlying feeling of greed and cowardice. Thanks for that, Donsis."

"Speaking of which: I lost everything when Hart left me for dead. I'm going to need to earn some coin," Donsis said, applying his money-loving talents.

"That depends. Do you wish to undertake a task that could very well change the fabric of reality?" asked Osiris, with a caution-filled voice.

"Wouldn't be the first-" Ash started, thinking back to the Drakeguard. But in the same breath, he declined Osiris' offer, seeking to rejoin his friends; too long had he rested in the Cult's care. "-however, I need to go back north. My friends might still draw breath."

"That's ridiculous, no one will survive Hart. I couldn't, you couldn't, and they won't," Donsis shot down.

"It was Wellington who crossed me. If it were Hart, he'd be the one sharing your pitiful life."

"Yet, here we sit, you and I. With no coins or favours to cash in on, Osiris is our only hope."

The elf spoke a rare truth, and Ash had no choice but to oblige. With a defeated nod, he accepted Osiris' request. Both had paid a costly price in the pursuit of Hericore's goals – now it was time to see what Osiris charged.

The old woman was pleased with their acceptance. Deep down, it was likely the only choice they had. Necromancers, unorthodox or no, tended to have a certain leash on their creations. Any animal would yield to an invisible collar.

"It's warming to see sense isn't lost on you. I need you and the other experiments to help my granddaughter."

"Your granddaughter? Hadn't pegged you as the married type," Ash said.

"More of the 'old crone' type," Donsis added, in a smug voice. The elf was quick to mock the woman who had saved them from a pair of painful deaths, yet she had little care for his petty remark and acted as if it was never uttered.

"My days of partnership ended long ago. I still keep him close, however," Osiris said, sombre and slow. In more sluggish actions, she retrieved a bundle of small scrolls from her deep pockets, and passed them across the table. "Days ago, my dear Natalia was contacted in her dreams. This was no illusionary force, but the presence of Lilith, Goddess of Death."

"Talk about a grim encounter," Donsis commented, having fear for the deadly goddess.

"We do not place fear in the mother of the end, unlike most people. We have faith in death, and this faith was rewarded in the form of a holy trial," Osiris explained.

Unrolling the scroll, Ash looked upon a map of Karin that was far cruder than Zarpadon's magical displays. "She's been ordered to travel south, simply south. Lilith commands it. Problem is, she's not a skilled fighter, and my fellow cult members are running a bit thin these days-"

"That's probably because I was doing a good job," Ash smirked.

"-so I made her three new warriors from the ruins of the old. You, Dallas, and the Beast."

The Beast, a name indicative of all necrotic creations. Ash and Donsis weren't rotten zombies or cheating symbiotes, but had still swerved the fatal grasp of the fatal goddess. Ash's new lease on life was a tainted one.

And still, Osiris kept urging them. "You must protect her – guide her. Then you can live your new life, free of debt."

"What debt?! I never asked for this," the dwarf exclaimed.

"You need not ask for rebirth. It is a reward given during the most dire of times."

"But we get paid at the end of this little quest, right?" Donsis said.

"If all you seek is wealth, I can compensate you, but only when my dear Natalia finishes her trial."

Shady and undignified business methods aside, the sound of jingling coins was too great for most men to turn down, and in Ash's case, he was more than just one man. If anything, helping a needy elder would be a feat in itself for him.

"I'll do it," Ash said, casting off his old life for the new one 'graciously' given. Donsis was quick in doing the same.

"Likewise."

Osiris face lit up with a successful look.

"Lilith praise. We shall discuss your payment for your service, Adonis."

"Ah, just call me Ash. I know I said Adonis earlier, but that's kind of stupid," he said, fighting off an innate argument to change his name along with the mission.

"Very well, Ash." Pulling a purse from her robes, Osiris threw the full bag on the table. "Two hundred silver casts, given on completion of Natalia's mission."

A pile of wealth he'd only see passed across the Council's table was now offered to him. It was enough to make a man sick, and he didn't need to think.

"Deal," Ash quickly replied, snapping at the high price so soon.

"Hold on now," Donsis intercepted. "We need more than that. Clothes to wear would be a start. And a down payment for food, water, you know: the essentials."

Another truth from the ever-dishonest elf. The month of Downpour was a refreshing one, but was cold at night, and nipped away at your fingers, toes, and other appendages.

"But of course. It would be criminal to allow you outside in nothing but a wolf-skin," Osiris agreed with a cackle. "I recovered all that I could from your bodies – weapons, clothing, and trinkets – all in a box outside by the tool shed. Given your quick recovery, I'd recommend heading out soon. Time waits for no man, not even those that cheat death."

Along with their old, damaged goods, the hag threw an extra twenty casts in. The greedy elf snagged quite the fair down payment.

"How long was I out, anyway?" Ash asked, slurping the remains of the porridge from the bowl.

"Ash, three days, the other, two. Why, are you missing something?"

"Our funerals, perhaps?" said Donsis.

By now, Wellington would've swept the Vitalands clean of Zarpadon and the others. It'd be an empty errand to go back, a notion Ash should have adopted sooner. He had to let go and embrace the concept of Adonis, and all it entailed. Only in reform could he earn back the valour he'd lost in Ester Valley.

"No, I don't think so. Not any more."

"Then step outside. My darling Natalia has already departed with the others, towards Roy's Folk," said Osiris, as she pointed to a partly unhinged wooden door. "Good luck, Adonis."

"I need the luck of Vita men, not necrotic hags," he mumbled, spitefully. He'd heard few words that were as much of a slight as Adonis, given the circumstance he was trapped in.

Even in this aspiring new life, suspicion followed. It hung over Osiris' crumbled mantle. Never trust those who'd one day float as corpses in the deep seas of heaven.

"Two heads are better than one," Donsis continually reassured himself, as they moved outside into the bright, sunny world.

For Ash, he found it interesting to see where this rebirth would drive him in his new, shared vessel – to riches or ruin.

Chapter 14: Land of the Rising Sun

Philip rode across the dusty plains of Karin with Thomas at his side and Langdon at his back. They were minutes away from Declandale, a small town close to the border. It was one of twelve small trade towns erected in Karin's northern region: the Freelands.

Like the other eleven towns, Declandale was named after its founder, or in its unique case, it was named after the twin founders. Though the brothers had passed long ago, their claim on this planet lived on, having quite the reputation.

Groups all over the Freelands met in Declandale to perform all manner of disreputable deals and trades – its isolation was a blessing in disguise. The town's lawless nature was the reason Philip chose to regroup and resupply here, over Hericore's alternative.

North Karin was unlike the rest of the dry lands, its inhabitants vastly varied, making for a healthy melting pot of culture. More of a savannah than a desert, the Freelands teemed with prides and packs of fauna, roaming the red sands endlessly. It was a wildlife enthusiast's paradise. That, or a hunter's twisted fantasy.

The road into town was lined on either side with thirsty, but still living shrubs and weeds, battling for what precious water they could salvage from the scorched earth. Unpaved and coarse, the roadway itself was raised almost a foot above the dusty plains that covered the remaining scenery.

Philip almost felt bad for the remaining Drakeguard and their eventual hike across the sandy ocean, surfing on waves of heat. The land had never been this harsh on his former visits. Maybe Magnus was conspiring against them? Mother Nature was ever the merciless bitch.

Still in the distance, Declandale stood, and at its core it was still the same as when he'd last ventured to this slice of southern comfort. Wooden shacks still crowded around the town's only water source – a well that was far over-pumped – and the dynamic nature of frontier towns was evident in the ever moving exterior settlements.

With hundreds of folks visiting every week, the ring of tents around the permanent residence never looked the same on a return visit. Like liquid, tents were erected and pulled apart all over the place; a flow of buyers, sellers, and scum.

"Man, I'm thirsty. They better have opened a milk bar in this dust bowl," Philip said, pursing his cracked lips.

"Milk? You still enjoy suckling at your mother's teat?" Thomas shunned.

"You'll swill back whiskey like water, but don't drink milk?" Langdon questioned. The silver knight rested under their cart's covers alongside the hoes. A journey short as theirs required little rest, yet Langdon spent his time under covers, regaining lost strength.

"Tom dislikes the idea of us milking one of his own," Philip explained.

"That's not true, Phil. It's just weird; whether cow, man, or both. Who the hell decided to grab an udder till it leaked, only to drink what came out?"

"A hero, that's who," Langdon said.

"Freak's more like it."

The best leaps in history came from heroes. Milk – in Philip's head – was one of these leaps. He drew inspiration from milk. Both were pale, thin, and underestimated by the average man. Finding power in the bottom of a glass was common for most, but not in the same manner as he. Philip truly was one of a kind.

"Don't disown the product because of its source. If that were the case, no one would eat eggs, or wipe their asses with synn leaves," he said, scolding Thomas' taste.

"Whatever. All I'm interested in is the booze, anyhow. Have your milk." shrugged the minotaur.

"Because that's better than milk?" Philip said disapprovingly. "Anyway, don't lose focus. We need to procure some Morphos and water skins. The boss isn't far behind."

"But you just yammered on about milk barns. How's that focused?"

"Because I'm the leader of this duo, and I can talk about milk all – damn – day!" In the disagreement, they slowly pulled up to Declandale's inn. "The Bled Lizard? Charming name," Philip observed, as Thomas saddled up the horse, and Langdon made his way inside the rather homely inn.

The Bled Lizard was raised off the ground and rough at the edges, a new addition to Declandale's hotspots. The interior was nice enough, with resplendent, cushioned seats made of baobab scattered all around the room's edges, which Philip could respect. Decorating the inn must've cost a few bassies, between the cooling blue flames and the ornate chandelier that held them, the Lizard looked better than any of Valordolt's dank domiciles.

The inn was grand in scope, but pitiful in execution. Longing for milk, Philip ordered just that, in addition to a plump roll for an early lunch. Faultless, the milk tasted fresh from the udder, and he quarrelled not. But the roll? Bread had never tasted so dry. While Thomas and Langdon settled down, he remained standing, tired of barren wastes forming in his mouth.

"Gods, this bun taste like sawdust. Hey barkeep, does your cook double as a carpenter?" he complained. Sure enough, he received daggers in the barkeeper's replying stare.

The man was a Karinese easterner, with dark skin, but light, pink lips. His body was gaunt, bar his broad shoulders. The suit worn over said shoulders was cheap, with far more work pumped into the Lizard's luxury furniture.

"These were made by my beloved daughter. She's a beauty, and puts love and care into each bite." The keeper raised a good point. Unfortunately, beauty and love didn't mean much to Philip's fickle appetite.

"Love doesn't make good buns, skill does. Now, I want a refund. *Comprende*?"

"A refund on a half eaten bun? I don't think–"

Philip tried to hold back, but after a long few days his grit teeth could only hold out for so long under the pressure of a hundred fake smiles. "Don't think then. *Do!*"

He felt bad for the poor man, but then again, he also wept for his fallen taste buds. It took a minute more, but the barkeep came round.

"I'm so sorry, sir. Here, have a few drinks too. With compliments."

And just like that, Philip's strong-armed tactics won the day again.

Not finished with the skinny barman, he rented a couple of rooms before joining his party on a corner table, looking out on the barren town. He placed their remaining funding on the baobab surface.

"That was unwise. Fighting with a man offering you shelter is often a bad decision," warned Langdon.

"Eh, I shouldn't have eaten that bread, but hey, life's all about making bad decisions." The knight's advice wasn't unfounded; Philip just didn't care enough to adhere to its moral. "Anyway, we have a hundred bassies left to not only stock the food and water, but the Morphos too. It's not looking good, folks," he sighed, counting up the stacks of gold hexagonal coins.

"I'm sure we can come to an arrangement with the traders," Thomas said, in an overly aggressive tone.

"And that's why you're staying here while I do the talking. Here, take these and buy a few more cold ones." Philip gifted some of Hart's looted silver to Thomas, and left the table.

"What about me?" Langdon asked.

"What about you?"

"I want to help you; return all you've done for me."

An odd gesture for a hired blade. Charity wasn't a strong suit of the disenfranchised. Langdon must've had an angle, likely pertaining to the hefty amount of bassies he's just counted.

"A noble offer, but what of your brother?" Philip questioned.

"And our pay," Thomas gurgled through a pint of bitter mead.

"Both waiting outside of town. I'll move out when night falls to meet him; there's far more safety under cover of darkness. For now, the day's all yours."

"Right. Well then, keep up," Philip warily agreed. "I could always use a pack mule.

"Be careful – this mule can kick." Langdon followed him outside, giving a Caster goodbye. "*Bonvo*, Thomas. See you around."

This mule can kick. Philip never doubted this, but for all the paranoia he felt towards the knight, he remembered Hericore's imparted words of wisdom. 'The storms of judgement can cloud even the brightest of minds', he'd say. Over time, this became a phrase Philip exercised with Langdon's idyllic disposition.

***

It was reaching midday, and the scalding rays from the sun pierced Philip's pasty skin harder than any weapon could. Longing for the succulent release of water draining into his mouth, he hurried over to the local trading post, situated at the high-street's western end.

"Gods this heat is unbearable. Back home was never this bad," Philip moaned, stopping beneath the shadow of Declandale's water tower. The tower's shade was only a temporary respite, but a welcomed one.

"Are you kidding?" Langdon smiled, basking in the sun. "Where do you think I gained my golden glow? A tan could do you a world of good, Phil."

"That or I'll scorch like a vampire at noon. Anyway let's keep moving. I wanna get this over with," he ordered. His hope was to have all of Hericore's menial chores done before the drake would arrive in the dust bowl.

However, thing were never that simple and all was not right. The shop had been pilfered of its stock. The door was knocked off the hinges, and two people stood in the busted frame, one a grey haired worker, and the other someone Philip never expected to see in this lone corner of the world. The second gent was a Greycoat, a detective for hire, operating out west.

As their name suggested, sleuths who worked under the Greycoat's moniker wore a dim trench coat, blank of any sign or symbol of what they stood for – not even the company's own banner. Operating under the 'grey man' hypothesis, the goal of these investigators was to not be recognised by anyone on their incognito missions.

This worked – for a time – but now the coat meant more than any sigil could, working in reverse by drawing in attention. Hypothetical hiccups aside, members of the organisation were very talented at their job. If one was present in Declandale, then something bigger than Philip was here.

The sleuth spoke in a sleazy western voice, thick with ill pronunciation straight from the Casterlands: a Waster-Caster accent. Through the cheap speech he was raised with, the detective used a sophisticated vocabulary, and clearly hated his sly accent.

Slim and clean, the man was like Langdon, only in an over-sized coat, not a suit of silver. The detective's hair was well coiffed and slicked back, with the 'stache on his lip mimicking a pencilled line of black hair. Along with fat hands and gangly legs, this Greycoat looked more like a caricature than a man.

The most notable part of this 'sketchy' sleuth was the nose, a wide and long proboscis that seemed unnaturally pointed; a triangle sticking out of otherwise flat head. With a nose so big, it was no wonder his slick voice had a nasally base.

The sleuth held a crumpled fedora in his left hand and a filled notebook in his right; the classic arsenal for a man who worshipped fact over faith.

"I need more than that, Arthur. It'll be impossible to catch 'em without any distinct feature of some kind," said the detective, sounding frustrated with the shopkeeper.

"It happened so fast. They were tall and broad in the shoulders," said Arthur, panicked and breathless.

Philip respected the moral goodness of a Greycoat, a life of protecting those too weak to act themselves. It was a path he'd sought once until he was dissuaded by the Order's impressionable youth.

"I can help," Philip said, a bold introduction to the pair. "Call me Philip, and this here's my muscle, Langdon."

The detective sneered at first, eyeing him up and down – Langdon too. He took no offence. It was a Greycoat's job, and the man eventually returned the pleasantry.

"Afternoon, fellas. Folks round town call me, the Bloodhound, but I'd prefer it if you'd use my real name, Rick Morello... or Patrick if you're feeling fancy. I never cared for it."

"Bloodhound? How'd you earn that name?"

Rick smiled and flared his nostrils. "That hint obvious enough?"

"Some say he can smell the very fear in your bones," said Arthur.

Rolling his eyes, Rick didn't agree.

"And those people are idiots. Inflating your ego is sad. Wasting your time inflating another man's? That's just moronic."

It wasn't hard to see how Rick had earned his place as a Greycoat. The position required a degree of humility and the grace of self-awareness, both things the man displayed effortlessly.

"Great. Nicknames aside, we need to slip past into the general store," Philip requested.

"Go ahead," Arthur sadly said, welcoming them into a room of ruin. "This ten foot square of raided junk is all that remains of my store, my livelihood, and Declandale's economy."

The damage was worse than Philip originally perceived. Everything that held value was taken, even a once bountiful pile of bedrolls.

"It was whisked into the desert without a trace. Been a long day for us both," Rick told him.

"Any culprits? Witnesses? Tracers, maybe? You checked for arcane tracers, right?" Philip questioned, tapping into long buried investigatory skills.

"Yes, but that's not for the ears of a traveller."

"Aww, come on. A man with no ties in this town, a large pool of human resources, and with a mutual interest in finding your criminals? That's exactly what you need."

Far as allies went, he trusted Rick over any other man in town, and gaining a Greycoat's help would be invaluable – far and above Hericore's prisoners.

Rick grinned, planted his hat atop his head, and humoured a reply.

"Fine, kid. You want to help? Follow me. I may have a use for you and that silver knight of yours."

With the enlightening feeling of accomplishment fresh in his mind, Philip waved Arthur adiéu and marched behind Rick to a quaint shack on the periphery of Declandale's residency.

Water was the key to surviving in Karin's deserts, and that meant Hericore needed water to execute his plan. As was the norm, Philip took on a burden that would break lesser men and tackled it head on. Not for honour, but for *her* safety, and by proxy, the world's safety also. For a world without his beloved wasn't a world worth saving.

Chapter 15: Growing Pains

Ash made his way to the rendezvous with Natalia and Osiris' other experiments. Armed with nothing but his trusty cleave rend and direction, his newly found nerves were running high.

The armour he was married to had been destroyed at the Order's hand, but his coat and bulky, militant boots scraped through intact. These were worn alongside Donsis' finely-tailored suit, keeping both fashion choices alive and well.

Their venture to the Fork was desolate, with not a single soldier or farmer in sight along the country roads; the dirt paths were stamped and broken, but devoid of travellers. Walking the lonesome road, Ash revelled in the grey skies and marshy fields of flood. These were signs of the Vitalands and its grim beauty, signs he'd been away from for a while.

The unenthusiastic chirps of soaked birds tweeted a sound chorus, but reminded him of a harrowing change: he was no long a man of Vitality. Now, life was nothing but a distant warmth in Ash's past, and much like the weak light piecing few clouds, grey now ruled his world.

Holding the smell of greenery in the air, this stretch of farmland was close to Valordolt, but crept around the main roads. Walking on a cracked path of stone, he wonder why so little care was lavished on these quaint pathways anymore.

Rain from days past gathered in the potholes, a dozen bricks upturned and taken by some poor builder seeking only to craft his home. Some trees also suffered this fate; giants wielding equally sized axes would fell them in one swoop. Since Vita's purge, the lowly population of the Vitalands seemed to follow the Order's lead; a land of people willing to sacrifice nature's beauty for their own needs.

But even when blemished, the view was a soothing one. Wind gently ran across the hills and across Ash's face, whistling a soft tune in his ears. Still, with his new partner rattling on the inside, comfort was a virtue no longer attainable.

"Can you believe those Order swine stole my shoes?" Donsis said, breaking Ash's introspection.

It wasn't a stretch. Boyd was known for being a meek kleptomaniac; paired with paranoia, Boyd Loyce was a problem just waiting to happen.

"You'll get over it. We have more important things to worry about."

"Yes, like what birthday we use?" Donsis said, acting the child again. "You can't just use yours, that's unfair."

"Unfair? This is *my* body. If you don't like it, take a hike."

"Ha, very funny. Look, if I'm going to be stuck in your filthy form for the rest of my days, at least use my birthday."

Ash had been part of Donsis for an hour, and already the elf was too much of a burden. Every sentence seemed to be tailored in hopes of annoying him.

"Why does it even matter? Just do 'ena mena mona mite,' or something. Hell, do you know how crazy I look, right now? To passers-by, I'm talking to myself," he asked.

"Correction: how crazy *we* look. No one knows I exist anymore, but I still share any knocks to our reputation, thank you very much," Donsis sulked. "Besides, I've never enjoyed my ears burning under scrutiny."

"Speaking of which, do you ever clean those big ears of yours?" Ash doubted, fishing a large nugget of discoloured wax from his newly grafted elven ear. Having another person's liver was unsettling enough, but the ear was ill-matched and looked ridiculous.

"Don't touch that. I don't want these dweller hands touching me."

"It's not my fault Hart destroyed that beanpole you called a body. Now make yourself scarce and return to the back of my head, like the afterthought you are," he said, trying his damnedest to force Donsis away. After some headache, he successfully held off the elf, and continued moving west towards the Fork.

It was a small but key part of any wanderer's journey around the Vitalands. Being located at the crossroads of three main settlements of Valordolt, Lumber's End and Ryford, the Fork was the start of the Order's rule, and remained secure to this day. Osiris' instructions were hazy, but Natalia had to be close. All wayward souls end up flocking to this humble trading post.

Donsis continually screamed and bellowed within, making Ash's lobes feel worn. Even walking became a strenuous task – he had to unchain the elf.

"See, Ash? Letting me talk is much more beneficial for the both of us. Suppression is never the answer, no?" Donsis taunted, as he continued to rant on about birthdays.

Another few long minutes went on, and without an end of Allisteel's jawing squabbles in sight. Ash stopped and humoured the annoying passenger.

"Fine, I'll use your birthday from now on. Does that shut you up?"

"Whoo hoo, you best get used to receiving your gifts on St Hayley's Day, Ash."

After hearing the elf mockingly laugh for a second, Ash gave a heavy pause and even heavier sigh.

"Are you shitting me?!"

Donsis paused from his victorious crowing. "What?"

"My birthday already falls on St Hayley's Day! We just wasted ten minutes fighting over nothing you stupid pr–"

"Who in lord Gideon's name are you talking to?" asked a deep voice from behind them.

Standing there was a gruff woman with boyish, blonde hair, and a large scar across her face. The wound stretched from the middle of her forehead, to the purple bags under her left eye, then down her flat cheek.

She was taller than Ash, or even Donsis' old body; she looked down on them with an inquisitive scorn. Her hairy hand was placed firmly on a sheathed weapon underneath a draping, wool cloak of white. The wool was pure, similar to the snowy silks of the north, and she wore it in a cautious stance, careful not to reveal too much.

Donsis panicked and retreated inwards, leaving the dwarf to explain his abnormal behaviour.

"You heard that, aye?" he asked, going red in the face.

"Whole bloody woods probably heard you. Are you a fractured one?" the woman countered with unease.

"No, I'm not crazy. I know it looks weird, but I'm not a fractured one."

"Well, you kinda are." Donsis resurfaced to spite his narrative.

"You don't sound so good," she replied, lowering her hand from the sword. Ash felt in good company, but what he thought wasn't all that mattered any more.

"I'm just lost. Looking for Roy's Fork," he struggled. "Is it near?"

"Just follow the road, it'll get you there."

She pointed her meaty fingers past the pair, showing off a patch of deep brown hair along her forearm, mismatching her sandy hair. With a broad frame of thick bones and skin, she appeared to be an ill-proportioned freak, much like himself.

"Why are you heading to the Fork? You look like you need a doctor," she wondered, examining his poorly-sewn patchwork.

"Oh, this?" Ash replied, pointing out Donsis' ear. "This isn't mine. I'm just... holding it for a friend."

"You're just holding an ear for a friend?" the woman asked doubtfully, moving back to her sword.

Donsis fought for control, wanting to run and hide, but Ash stayed resilient and kept the coward from bailing. If this brutish broad wanted to fight, he welcomed a challenge, allowing him to hone skills that had become rusty in death. But Allisteel clung to the dissenting opinion.

"I'm going to leave now. Run, actually. Don't follow me, please," Donsis whimpered.

"Your voice. It changes," she said, perplexed by the bi-polar nature of Adonis.

"No!" Donsis roared, poorly impersonating Ash's own, burly voice. "It never changed... *mate*? The grog's talking, is all."

Ash pushed for control of the body, attempting to quell the embarrassment that Donsis was breeding. Streaks of electric pain shot down his spine to every tip of every fingers, a jolt that caused his entire form to writhe sporadically. The mental war took its toll, and within seconds of fighting, the pair entered a fugue state of incompatibility.

The woman just stood there, confused, as the duo dropped to the floor with a bang and began to toss and turn on the ground, violently mumbling about wardens and time stones. Not their proudest moment.

"Great. I think I've found him!" she shouted, and started to haul his twitching body off the road, over to some stranger in the tree line.

***

Hours passed, and Ash opened his eyes from his mental anguish to see a thing of pure physical anguish: a great creature of terrific agony loomed ahead.

It was the product of experimenting too far, and it showed on the warped flesh-stick. Flesh, fur, and scale worked in tandem, from toothy chest, to a tail made of a blind snake's body.

Its front legs were that of a large wolf, both decayed, with some parts only chipped chunks of bone. The hind legs were hooves, likely from a horse. Between the pairs of legs were several other limbs – human in nature; they too were decayed, and sat asymmetrical from each other, one on the right and two on the left.

The beast smelled worse than he looked, not that it would know. Despite having three heads, none of them shared a nose. Perhaps as a mercy?

Head one was wrinkled and warped prior to death, with a thick moustache drooping low. The second head was perched beside the first, younger and remorseful. The last was a growling, canine skull, angry till the end. This last head had a second pair of eyes fused to it, slanted and lidless.

The monstrosity whimpered, pained by its very existence, wailing with great conniption.

It was the most savage concoction of man and beast Ash ever seen, and he shuddered just to hear its cries, instilling genuine fear that was, for once, not a product of Donsis. He reacted to this ghastly hulk on the elf's behalf, backing up against the nearest tree, shaking and at a loss for breath.

To the creature's right was the gruff woman from before. She knelt by a small fire, stirring a cast iron pot with care.

"Calm down, dwarf, he doesn't bite," she calmly said. "You're the third patchwork, right? The one Osiris said was gonna càtch us up?"

"He doesn't bite? That seems like a lie," Ash shuddered.

"It is. And you haven't answered my question. Are you the third patchwork?"

"That I am. Ash Belwert, at your service."

"Well Ash, you're lucky we heard your mental breakdown. If not, you would've passed right by the very people you sought," she smiled, pouring a dense portion of Bluvon Opi into the pot. "I'm Dallas, by the way, and this handsome devil is the Beast"

The Beast seemed rather unresponsive, and just twitched his head back and forth repeatedly, like he was scanning the woods for something – predators or prey. Ash couldn't imagine how fried the Beast's mind must be.

"Aren't you going to introduce me?" questioned Donsis, confusing Dallas again.

"Sure. Dallas, Beast, this is Donsis," Ash said, and with shame he pointed to the ear. "He's the one I was fused with. Bit of an arse really."

"Wow. You got to keep your friend's personality?" asked Dallas. She lost her own proud stature, and frowned extensively. "Wish I was given the same blessing. God's gifts are sparse, I suppose."

She removed her cloak, and showed a man's body underneath the wool disguise. Her abnormal size was no freak twist of nature or a difficult life choice.

With another deep scar ringing around her neck, it was obvious where the woman ended and the man she was stitched on to began. Ash wondered who she was fused with. A friend? A sibling? A lover? All poor options.

"If you don't mind me asking..." Donsis began, but Ash cut off the moronic elf before another chance to soil their reputation slipped out.

"Where's Natalia? Isn't she the leader of this here crew?" Ash asked.

"She's doing her 'business' somewhere that way," Dallas said. She pointed north, through a thick grouping of sycamores. "Being the only woman here with... well... woman parts, she wanted to go off alone."

Donsis couldn't contain himself, and not even Ash could control his arrogance.

"Well, that answered my query. You *do* have a tallywhacker!"

Dallas gave him an unhappy raised eyebrow, and confirmed the blunt remark.

"Yes. Part of the surgery," she answered, filled with unease at the though.

"Sorry about that," Ash added. "Like I said, Donsis is an arse."

"No worries. A patched partner seems to be a blessing and a curse. To make things plain and simple, I have no tits either, case you'd be wondering. Not the female kind anyway. Everything from the neck down was axed." Solidifying this, she made a slow, slicing gesture across her neck scar.

This little crew of patchwork soldiers was an odd one. Now more than ever, Ash missed his companions from the Drakeguard. For all their shortcomings and arguments, the Guard was one heck of a family. Even

Philip's cocky half-smile was a thing to reminisce over. He'd have to discover their fates... someday.

"How bizarre," Donsis commented, "I once knew a–"

In a sudden flurry, a loud, shrill scream echoed from the north, alerting the trio.

"That sounded like Natalia!" Dallas panicked.

"Maybe business is a little hot and heavy – if you catch my drift," Ash suggested.

"Maybe we should stay here and wait it out," Donsis added. The elf had an admirable amount of cowardice, a brand so intense that it redefined the very meaning of the word.

"To Tarus with that! I'm not risking her life. Stay if you must, but I need her," Dallas said, marching north with the Beast.

"I'll be right behind you," Ash said, disregarding Donsis' fears.

The dim sunlight under the tree line was scarce, and finding Natalia's distress was a challenge in its own right. Eventually, they located the cry, and found Natalia clinging to a low sycamore branch, as a savage stalker tried to claw at her from the trunk.

It was a woodland beast known as a florankhi. Ankhi were creatures that evolved to blend into their environment, so well that most forget their true nature: to kill and consume. The florankhi was a breed native to the Vitalands, with bark skin and a leafy bush for a mane. Beneath said mane was a set of sharp, ivory teeth that could rip a bear to pieces, and its claws were even more deadly.

He'd faced one before, accidentally mistaking the thing for a bed of shrubbery while wandering drunk around the Warrens – the second biggest mistake of his life. Last time, he'd fled from the mass of leaves and sticks, but here he was, forced to rescue his new boss from an ivory hell.

Natalia's fear shook the young sycamore, and hundreds of its winged seeds fluttering around the woods. They twisted softly to the earth, spinning past the frenzied florankhi.

"Kill this forsaken thing!" screamed Natalia, clinging for dear life, the florankhi's claws brushing up against her discoloured armour.

She had an odd sense of fashion, pairing armour with cloth in all the wrong ways. Although protection covered her arms and legs, a hardy material that had similar colours and faded gleam to that of bone, she kept her torso and all the vitals inside free from restriction, ultimately making her an unpackaged meal for the florankhi.

Over her body were loose robes, tangling her in nearly a foot of slack. Dyed purple, they showed off a little too much, particularly her chest. Ash never knew mages tailored their robes in such a low-cut manner. This served as a scant reminder that she wasn't just a mage, much like her grandmother. Necromancers always were rebels, even down to their attire. Luckily, Osiris hadn't worn such a dress.

"Is that some kind of tree dog?" questioned Dallas.

"Tree dog? Seriously?" Donsis said, both baffled and amazed by her ignorance.

"What would you call it, then?"

"It's a florankhi. We can help her, lest our task ends before it begins," ordered Ash.

The florankhi's cry was that of chirping birds, made to attract prey instead of scare them away. Opposing the light tweets of the floral lion was the animalistic roar of the Beast – all noise and fury in his cry. The Beast didn't hold back either – without a second though he charged at the florankhi and tackled it far from Natalia.

Dallas stood under the tree and yelled, "I got you." But Natalia refused to let go; her fear was strong, and her grip equally so.

Ash wanted to take his cleave rend and chop the bark monster's head clean off, but Donsis was acting up again.

"Come on, Donsis, work with me for once," the dwarf gritted out.

"No, no, no, not against *that*. It's like a squirrel mated with a plant weaned on quint dust."

"If you don't sit back and let me handle this, then Natalia's gonna die, and her blood is on my hands. Not yours, mine!"

The Beast's grotesque claws ripped at the florankhi's bark, tearing at the brown flesh beneath. With equal aggression, the bark creature fought back, and its thorned tail whipped at the Beast, tearing his stitches and opening his wounds, causing a painful, echoing roar.

"Help me to help them!" Ash begged Donsis.

"Fine. But I'm choosing dinner... if we survive this mess," Donsis bargained, as he relinquished control.

"Deal."

The resilient florankhi welcomed the extra combatant, and became more mobile, weaving in and out of the undying warriors, slowly weakening them, blow by blow. Ash landed a couple of hits himself before being pounced on by the animal. Holding off his snapping jaws with the handle of his render, Ash could feel the warm, piny breath of the monster inches from his face.

"Ash, kick our right knee straight up," Donsis said from his objective position in the fight.

Since options were limited, he complied, and rammed his knee into the florankhi's open stomach wounds, forcing the creature back in pain. Dallas finished the scrap by thrusting her blade through the monster's chest, killing it once and for all. The battle died, along with Ash's energy, his aches and pains moving into more than just his mind.

"That... That was close," Dallas said, catching Natalia from the tree and cleaning the blood off her blade. "Good work with the knee. I'd never have thought of that."

"Two heads, right?" Ash said, tapping his noggin and thanking his passenger.

Natalia brushed the dirt and leaves off her purple robes.

"Thank you, all of you. That would've been my end. An end ill-fitting for someone of my authority."

"How'd you piss off a florankhi? They're quite the indifferent sops, these days."

"I was looking for a makeshift outhouse, and may have mistaken it for a bush," admitted Natalia, her cheeks reddened.

"Seriously?" asked Donsis. "That's so stupid, I can't even–"

"Now is not the time for mockery. Beast is badly wounded," blocked Dallas. With the Beast leaned over her for support, his whimpers were now that of a wounded pup.

"Let's get back to the camp, I've got some stitching there," ordered Natalia, "and we can have a catch up... Ash?"

"Adonis," Ash corrected. "What?! No, not Adonis. I'm... Ash."

The battle had left him lacking lucidity. Colours faded and grey wasn't limited to the sky. He needed more Opi.

When the four returned, they found the campfire reduced to embers, and the pot above was filled with a black broth of charred ingredients. Natalia searched through her belongings for a vial of clotted red liquid, and nursed Beast back to health, bottle feeding him like the pup he impersonated.

"Damn, the broth's ruined," said Dallas, poking the cremated dish with a stick.

"We could cook that florankhi: become one with it. Most of it is edible," suggested Natalia.

"Nah, I'm good. Never liked greens in the first place," Ash said. "Let's just go. Can't be more than a few miles from the Fork." He attempted to march on, but collapsed under exhaustion's weight.

"First, Adonis, you need stop exerting yourselves. Unity comes with some of grandmother's Bluvon Opi. It's a family recipe–"

"I know, I know. Just gimme a bottle and get it over with. I ain't used to being an addict."

The purple ooze was comforting, not in taste, but in effect. In minutes, the world's colour returned and Ash was whole. Wiping away the foul taste, he followed his Cult to the Fork, Royland's original rest.

Chapter 16: The Hunt Begins

Hart let the state of his office decay. No clean-up crew was called in to take care of the mess Donsis made on the way out, and he demanded solitude for rest of the night.

Reluctantly, he admitted the comfort of spilt blood around him, unbridled in its entirety. A craven on the surface of Magnus, Donsis was a problem that would never come back, and that pleased him. If only the same could be said for Kenneth.

The key difference in Hart's mind was Kenneth's agency compared to Donsis'. Unlike the elf, Kenneth wasn't an independent fellow, always a player in someone else's game. Back in Betiel, the lowly fisherman had nothing held against his name, and that led to one conclusion: he was a cut-out, a pawn in a match far greater than his own.

Whether Kenneth killed Hart's family under another's orders or under the constraints of mental illness, he was not to blame for the crime. That was the only reason the fisherman had been spared the block. The dog's master had let him loose, and now the rabid fool roamed the world freely. This was a humiliation that Hart couldn't wipe off, even with a thousand pints of Donsis' blood.

The black letters were ash, housed in the hearth rather than in the palms of grieving widows and parents alike. This would be his final act of charity to the people of Valordolt before he broke away to Karin and reunited with the mongrel.

The more he looked over the red on his pale hands and the red on his blue jacket, the more his sentiment wavered, however. By the time his newly appointed superior had arrived, Hart was walking the line of kill and capture – a dangerous place to be if your name was Kenneth Porter.

Maybe the almighty above would show compassion and return Anya to him if such kindness was shown to Porter? It wasn't unheard of, and a bargain like that could save his very soul. But it all seemed too distant, a far-fetched feeling that manifested in the dark, cavernous regions of his heart.

"Sir," Lud addressed him, peering into the room.

The thunderous clapping of horseshoes on cobbles bounced around the entire prison, and meant one thing. His overseer had arrived. 'Replacement' was far more appropriate, as without the chase, Hart couldn't have Kenneth, and without Kenneth, he could stomach the title of Warden no longer.

"Yes? What is it? I'm rather absorbed right now," he answered in a tired voice.

"Your new boss has arrived."

"Yes, I could gather as much. What I want to know is: who is he?"

Hart expected a high-up commander, hand-picked from Wellington's core strike force. Someone who could level a fortress, but also lead men with honour and civility.

"It's… um… Hunter, Sir."

"What! This is a joke in poor taste, no?" Hart asked. His face returned to a familiar shade of red.

"No, I wish it was, Sir. The quiver-toting boy is prancing around the courts like he owns them."

The gods weren't compassionate, what was he thinking? Hunter now owned the courts as judge and jury, a mockery in the face of all Hart had fought for.

"Hunter's not fit to lead a squad of schoolboys, let alone my jailers," he spat. "What's he doing?"

Lud clenched his fists, sharing in the rage.

"He's ordering around Jelz and Boyd like they're his own."

"And his pack of poorly-trained rubes?"

"Twelve of 'em. All hunters, like the boy himself."

Hart couldn't allow a kid to run his hunt, even with such an appropriate title backing him.

"I want you to round up every jailer on duty and send them to the yard. I'm relieving Hunter of his service," Hart hissed.

"You'd kill him?" said Lud, shocked at the idea.

"No, but he can spend the night in a cell instead of hindering my mission. Now get moving!"

The Warden hobbled out to meet the kid head on. Fitting his role, Hunter was already busy loading up the party of trackers, ready to lead the group south. The time had come for Hart to reclaim order in the Order, and break a poorly strung chain of command.

Hunter detected him from across the yard and offered him a warm greeting. Returning nothing short of a tundra-cold stare, Hart made sure the kid's welcome was far from friendly.

"Percy! Glad you could shuffle your senior hide down here in time for the departure. A feat for you, I'm sure."

Wearing a crooked smile with the same inadequacy as the poorly-fitting suit on his shoulders, Hunter was asserting himself too hard.

"Only two people are allowed to call me Percy and walk away with a full set of teeth; you are neither," Hart replied, shrugging off the boy's mirth, putting hostility in its place.

"Prolly both just as miserable as you. I'd love to meet these poor, poor souls," Hunter smirked.

Without a mention of mercy, Hart replied, "That can be arranged."

Their verbal trades became faster with each step they took, stopping mere feet apart at the request of another.

"Boss!" Boyd beckoned, standing between the two suited giants. "I warned him to act respectful, but–"

"That's quite alright. Hunter will learn his manners... one way or another. But for now, I'll gladly teach him an important rule to live by."

"That is?" Hunter said, lounging against a barrel of wine.

"Never stake a claim on my job unless you plan on retiring early."

"That's not a very useful titbit. Certainly not something I'd say to my new commander in chief." Hunter's men crowded around Hart and his captains, holding greater numbers and arms, but this didn't affect the Warden's stone-faced expression.

"I have no commander. I'm the Warden, the be-all and end-all in this place," Hart retorted. Lud arrived on scene with a dozen of his own men to match Hunter's, unnerving the boy.

"No commander? I think Dirk would prove otherwise," Hunter snarled. "She granted me this privilege, after all." Pulling a rolled up snippet of paper from his breast pocket, the kid read aloud in a condescending voice. "'Dear Percival. It has come to my attention that your antics regarding Kenneth Porter will turn you to ruin. I already have my suspicions over your involvement with the Belmont Bombing, and recommend you submit to Hunter and my orders immediately.' See? That's my claim to your throne,

Percy."

First this mysterious Kalsec bombed the tower, then Dirk blamed it on him? A stronger set-up had never reared its head. Though Hart's leg still throbbed in painful pulses, Hart stepped up to Hunter with a cold, unmoving look.

"That crooked witch has lusted for my head for a while now. You think she can pin the bombing on me? Better yet, do you think she hasn't sent more like you to wrangle me in the past? If you, like them, value freedom, it would be wise to back down," he threatened, without remorse. "Boyd, Jelz, and Lud are by my side, not yours. That's thrice the back-up I need to knock you back to the woodwork you crawled out from, boy."

With that, a dozen bowstrings cracked under the force of twelve drawbacks; the hunters were loyal, not taking kindly to the insult.

"Now, now, Percy, let's not bother with the utterly forced gestures of dominance. You and I are not happy about this arrangement, and that's okay." Hunter matched the weight that Hart was so quick to throw around. He had to commend the lad for the gall of his speech, a trait few held, and even fewer acted on. "But this display of yours needs to end. All good dramas have that final curtain call. Don't overstay this one."

"You're right, kid. This stare-down needs to end." Charging head first, the Warden aimed to plunge deep at Hunter's gaunt ribcage. What would follow was of no concern to him. A few lives lost now would save many later.

Hunter was no push-over, and ultimately proved to be the exact opposite. In five short seconds, the Warden was disarmed and sent to the ground with both a broken nose and pride.

"Too slow, old man. That brace is your downfall," the kid gloated, rallying his men to nock an extra arrow at Lud and the jailers.

Laying between two crowds of heated threats – the hunters and the watchers – Hart couldn't risk falling any further. All the defeat he'd feel at Hunter's hand meant nothing compared to the defeat of losing his own family. Never again.

"Hold your positions. All of you, keep those heads cool and attached to your shoulders. If this is my last order, I order you *not* to die for me," Hart commanded, and just like that, silence erupted. The quiet swiftly disappeared in the wake of the grinning hunter's next words.

"Loyal as ever, these boys of ours. Good. I'd of never live down their slaughter."

Hart leaned in close and shared a private plea with the elven lad, appealing to whatever empathy they shared.

"These are my men. Mine! You have *no* right to take them from *me*. Not like this," he begged angrily.

"You think that you're actually helping, don't you?" Hunter belittled with an overly dramatic frown.

"Yes."

"You'd never guess it, but I believe you," Hunter said, before tossing him back into the arms of the rangers. "And a wrong man who thinks he's right may be the most troublesome thing on this dying planet."

The rangers grasped at Hart's limbs and carried him away, all while Hunter goaded the jailers into defying him now. It remained a challenge that nobody met.

"I'm not going to let a jumped-up punk like you push me out of the biggest manhunt of the era. They're my prisoners!" Hart argued, fighting against the current of ranger that dragged him away.

"No. They're animals, as you so often say. And we both know I'm the man who hunts the animals," Hunter said, with a cheery wave. "Lads, take Percy to his new 'office'."

Hart had never liked mirrors. The sight of own image was too poor to bear, and now Hunter's newly found power was forming a mirror over his face – a rudimentary successor to his demented legacy as warden.

Tenacity was instilled in his bones, and he lashed out against the rangers that pulled on him, their arms like ropes around his neck, hanging his shame for all to witness. "And in case you didn't hear earlier: nice hair, Percy," Hunter called, and took a spectator's seat atop the wine barrel.

"At least I have hair, you bald tosspot!"

Nothing short of being beaten into submission, Hart was down and out. A decade of service was repaid with a broken body and a burning lust for revenge. Both festered greatly in his newly-appointed 'office': the old cell that once housed Donsis. The irony mocked his fall from grace.

***

In a matter of minutes, the grand revenge plot had crumbled into finer ashes than Hericore's plan ever did, and Hart was confined in the same deplorable conditions he'd subjected his prisoners to for years. Taking tips from his old mongrel Kenneth, he used hate and anger, attempting to cocoon into a numb husk focused on surviving, if only to make Hunter regret his words and actions one day.

By his design, the cells were meant to punish their tenants. With a cold temperature and atmosphere, they could slowly break down any man who dared to find false glory within their own imprisonment.

On the hour, every hour, one of his old lackeys peered in and flung all manner of names his way; from killer, to monster, to failure. When a man turned on his leader, that was the end of his lead.

Hart's stay in Refracted Light was short lived. Soon, he was visited by his own guardian angel in the form of Boyd.

"Hey, boss. How's it going?"

"How's it going? How do you fucking think?" he hissed. "I've been robbed. I'm a man denied his needs, forced to rot in a hell of his own creation."

"Okay, I get it: Hunter won. That much is *very* clear."

Hart felt his self-anguish grow out of control and sought to rectify it, lest he fall into the sorrowful abyss that consumed so many.

"Are you going to mock me like the others? Call me a soulless beast? Pelt me with mouldy bread and call it my supper?"

"Not at all. I'm here to ask you some questions," Boyd replied, pulling a tiny, rusted key from his pocket; the distinct key matching a cell lock.

Hart's weathered face cracked a tiny smile. "You're going to free me? That's my man."

"Like I said, I need to ask you some things first. If you answer me honestly, then the Council don't need to know about this whole incident."

If Boyd's task was to report to the Council on Hunter's behalf, and he'd not accomplished this already, then things were already set in stone. Fealty found its place quickly in the heart.

"If you plan on deceiving the Council, then I think my freedom is practically definite," Hart stated confidently. He and Boyd went back, way back. Covenants of order meant nothing to a bond so old – assuming the men behind it were as noble.

"Let's not get ahead of ourselves," Boyd said, retracting the key from view. Hart threw up his arms and surrendered to questioning.

"Fine. Ask away."

"If I let you out of this cell, how many more are going to die? Good, bad, innocent, and guilty. I want a number."

Hart briefly thought of saying only one: Kenneth. He knew Boyd wouldn't buy it, however.

"Ten – if all goes well. The prisoners, Hericore's traitors, and Hunter."

"And if it doesn't?"

"A extra dozen, if Hunter's men don't cooperate. I can't tolerate insubordination." He saw Boyd cringe at the answer. It was a sad reality, full of misfortune and happenstance that he would wish away if he could.

"Just one more question," Boyd pouted. "Why?"

Hart had no trouble answering this. So much time had passed since Kenneth had been captured, but that didn't lessen his motives. Not one day passed where Hart felt guilt or sympathy for the mutt, and this needed to be expressed.

"Boyd, you've known me for ten years. In those ten years, I've kept passive, not once has a man died to my hand. Things have changed. The life of peace I swore myself to? That needs to end. My one relief in this world has gone parading out of his home, his rightful place." Hart's soft tone grew, as he tightened his fists, forcing them to creak. "Until he's back in said place, I can't be the man you know. He, Hunter, and the others don't need to die, they *want* to die. Why else would they attempt to take my relief away? They're testing my resolve, hoping for the worst. And by the gods, I'm going to deliver! My blood for theirs!"

Without noticing, everything had become hazy, and he'd worked up into a red-raw rage, bellowing his words at Boyd's fearful stare.

"What did the Ripper do to you? What did he change back then, that's changed you right now?"

Hart gritted his teeth. "You said no more questions."

Boyd remained still, but eventually, he swallowed a plum of guilt and held the key to the lock, slowly but surely making his choice. Hart didn't know if it was done out of confidence in his words or the fear.

After ten years the captain's mind remained a mystery – even to Hart. A family man who lived alone, a tubby man who barely ate, Boyd's habits always contradicted themselves.

Strolling out of captivity, Hart stretched out his cramped limbs and got back on track.

"Guess this makes another breakout," smiled Boyd. "The Council's going to kill me."

"I doubt it. We will be long gone before Dirk's haggish snout catches a whiff of your betrayal."

Hart's disdain for Dirk had never been greater. It was said that the most devious and desperate ploys were concocted under the influence of disdain. If he were to return here, it wasn't going to be in chains. If the Order wanted a terrorist, he'd fit the boot they'd so generously provided.

Bart the Bold, a man who'd sought to make a mockery of Valordolt, never quite achieved his dream. As a warden of the same city, Hart was forbidden to idolise Bart's tenacity. However, he was no longer a warden.

"Boyd, do you remember where I sealed away Bart's possessions?"

"Bart the Bold? Why do you–"

"Just answer me. Where?"

"I dunno. I was just a rookie when Bart's head met the block"

"Most of it was handed to Tyber: a show of good faith. An exception is the rouge candle; it was a treasure far too valuable. I ditched it in the Vault... among other things."

Never had the ex-Warden been so happy in Refracted Light's walls. The rouge candle was a thing of pyromania, and Bart had lusted over it until his bloody end. After the Order carelessly painted Hart as the same, a man lusting over destruction, it was only fitting to take on that role. Tonight, if only as a fail-safe, he'd see the candle recovered from the basement's labyrinth. If he ever saw Dirk's face again, it'd warrant the candle's use, and its dark flare for chaos.

"Retrieve it, Boyd. We know not where Bart's bombs are placed, but I'm sure the Order will be hesitant to find out."

"Boss, that's madness. If it goes off..."

"Then Bart's dream becomes reality, and we get an easy escape... assuming Dirk wants to be persistent. Arrogant as he was, Bart's old plans still lie in wait. 'Code Black,' I believe he called it."

Hart's captain wasn't convinced. Regret covered Boyd's face, and only for an instant did it shift, but an instant was all he needed.

"Only as a last resort?"

"Only then. Our own Code Black."

Agreeing, albeit with hesitation, Boyd followed the order to the letter. The 'last resort' was set, and things were looking up. In one fell swoop, Hart was free, had managed to spite Dirk, and fulfilled the legacy of a fallen anarchist. All was good, for the moment.

But the lingering sense of unfulfilled duty remained. Kenneth was also sharing Hart's freedom, and he couldn't rest now; that was a luxury reserved for the good people of the world.

"Well, let's catch up with our friend Hunter. I can wait to... relieve him of his duties," he ordered. "Tonight the hunter will become the hunted."

Boyd collected some horses and equipment for them to ride away with, and Hart waved his corrupted city goodbye. He never planned on returning to the place that had kept him occupied for years. Not because of bad memories, but for a lack of good ones.

"This must make us outlaws now," Boyd said.

"I never stopped being an outlaw."

The Fifth's End turned many to the highwayman's code, Hart included. It was a rough life, but pleased him more than any night patrolling Betiel or warding Valordolt. Money, wine, meat, and blood were the four tenets he'd lived by in those days; all stopped by a woman.

This woman had no money, despised wine, and ate vegetables. In the end, the last tenet claimed her, and Hart only wished he'd been there to say goodbye.

"What will people think of us?" Boyd fretted. "My wife and children will know nothing of my true mission."

"They'll understand. They have to, it's what makes them family. Our ends will serve justice to our means, but until then, we must become lesser men. We can't beat the enemy unless we stoop to their level first, but aye, as is the way of life."

Chapter 17: A Nightmare in Black

Philip was swept away from his task by Rick, who filled his mind with present events in Declandale.

Between the annual droughts and infestations, the town was being pestered by a far bigger parasite than bugs and worms. A notorious yet elusive crew of bandits had arrived a year past, and had Rick tied up in all manner of cases, ranging from robbery to murder; a pleasant bunch, really.

A day passed them by. Langdon ventured to find his brother, and the next sun passed them by also. Rick taught Philip, and he impressed the detective. Joining the Greycoats would've suited him well, and he was more the fool for rejecting that path those years ago.

Langdon returned twice, once with an update on Thomas' drunken stupor, and again with dinner. The three men talked at length about all manner of things, eventually reaching the complexity of dreams and their dreamers.

Rick never dreamed, while Langdon always had a soft sleep, soaked in the pleasantry of heroic conquests – a life the knight could no longer have. Philip's own recollection of his 'dreams' wads forcibly vague, so as to shield his gift from the others.

But the silver knight's matching tongue wore Philip down, and he mentioned the recent plagues in his visions. First orange fires, now a crimson apple rotting from the inside out haunted his nights. Neither men believed it to be more than an over-active mind let loose, and the Time Stone remained out of their talks.

While Rick grabbed more case notes from the shack he dubbed an office, Philip, along with Langdon, waited patiently in the cramped space. A smell of spent tobacco filled the hastily built shanty, mixing with the travelling aroma from the sandy plains, overloaded Philip's nose with sickening scents of meat fit only for carrion.

'The Kennel' was the name of Rick's tiny slice of personal paradise, a fitting name for the old bloodhound, but didn't leave the right impression on Philip. He'd expected so much from the suave man, wrapped in a coat. This was a far cry from elegant or charming.

Langdon didn't make things any better, tapping away at the arm of his chair, burrowing the sound deep in Philip's head, like a tick. The pair sat in front of Rick, and a desk so large it ruled half the floor space, along with a couple of mismatched wooden cabinets.

Rick had no room for the basics. He couldn't see where the detective slept and ate – the place even lacked an outhouse, bringing more questions into Philip's head, already swelling with fresh knowledge.

Luggage, recently unpacked, gave the impression Rick was returning from a long journey. There were four cases in total, two of which were bigger than a dwarf. Wherever he came from, it seemed like a permanent departure. That, or the detective hoarded his wares; a theory that gained credibility the longer it took for Rick to organise the overflowing papers.

"Sorry to keep you boys waiting," Rick apologised, surfing through a wave of paperwork and stained folders. "Haven't had much time to make my workplace visitor friendly."

"You don't say," commented Langdon, tapping faster and faster.

"No worries, Ricky," Philip assured him; ever the counterbalance.

"The men and women responsible for the raids had a pattern before. They'd attack the tents far from Declandale's core: fewer eyes to witness their dark deeds. But now, the general store has broken that pattern," Rick was unhappy to admit.

The detective stumbled around the room again, frantically thinking in all directions. It was just like after Palmer; Zarpadon was a bumbling mess of nerves, back then. Admittedly, even Philip fell to the scope of what lay ahead. Hericore was the only member to keep a tempered head in the anarchy – a state that he'd kill to own.

Seeing into the future had its consequences in the form of an aching head. Not every day was a slog, but enough were. Looking back, too many were. Would his ends justify the means? Did they ever?

"Could it be a simple spike in confidence?" Philip suggested.

"Maybe. But I've put the squeeze on these mooks for months now. Kicked them out of two former bases of operations. Yet here they still stand, bold as brass."

"You become too confident, you start to make riskier moves. It's only natural," Philip said, speaking from experience. "That's how you'll catch these savages."

"Yes, but I can't just wait for them to slip up. Too many lives are in danger."

Philip looked off to his side and saw Langdon drifting away from the conversation. A being of action must loathe every second in this place; all talk and no walk.

"Stay with us, pal," he said, reminding the knight of the task at hand.

"Why? Give me a location, and I'll get those supplies back. It's that simple."

"It's not simple, not even close to simple. If I could give you a location this easy, I'd have done the deed weeks ago," Rick said, frustrated. "I'm banking on your fresh eyes. That and a little southern luck should shine new light in my search for these dogged bastards."

The bandits hid well. Finding their home would be difficult, but finding the bandits themselves? That was ease itself. A man could hide in the hills forever, but hiding from himself wasn't possible for long.

"You're asking the wrong question," Philip told Rick.

With a humoured chuckle, the Greycoat said, "Then what should I ask?"

"Not where, but *who*."

Without an answer, Rick ripped a sketch from his mountain of papyrus and slid it over to him.

"That a good enough who for ya?"

A grizzled face, weathered beyond its time, stared at Philip from the ink-spotted portrait; this was the man behind the madness. More scar tissue than unscathed flesh, with a black outrider cap covering his hair, the mere image was chilling.

"Out of the ten witnesses, eight painted this picture in my mind. The personification of callousness." The Greycoat was notedly pleased with Philip's innovative thinking, and after handing over the picture, made sure to praise him in such a way. Words such as 'a hero in the making' spilled forth from Rick's pursed lips, a saying Philip thought he'd never hear again; not since his youth had those words been uttered.

His childhood held little memory, but those words of encouragement never left him. It was those words that made him the man he was today, yet he never knew the man who spoke them. Only a dapper suit and tie reached out from the past, and it wasn't enough. Was it an uncle or cousin? Did he have either? Little room for the past still remained after he'd started to see the future.

"You drew this yourself?" Philip asked.

"I did. Being an artist was my second choice after being a crime fighter."

"Talent manifests in the most barren of places. Check it out, Langdon." Philip forced the sketch under his friend's nose, and Langdon perked up at once, finally dropping his sluggish attitude.

"This is..."

"Gorgeous, right?" he finished, actually impressed by the depressing art.

"My skills with ink aside, it brings us no closer to identifying 'Mr. Null'. He isn't local, so I doubt we'll find answers around town," Rick warned.

Philip hadn't seen this face in any of his dreams. It was refreshing to see a fresh mug these days. "What about your brother, Langdon? He lives nearby. Maybe he saw something out in the Barrens?"

The knight went silent again, and crumpled the sketch in his palm. With his voice gaining a malignant quality, Langdon groaned, "Oh, he'll know."

"What's wrong, kid?" Rick asked.

"We need to hunker down. Do you possess any weapons? We'll need them."

"Course: an old revolver in my drawer." Rick sounded panicked, and Philip felt the same, but Langdon didn't. Keeping a level head, the knight's questions continued.

Moving to the shack's lone window, Langdon's questions continued.

"Philip. Your friends will be here soon?"

It didn't sound right, and the fake hopelessness in his words struck Philip with suspicion. It was here, at the twilight of failure, that Philip's heart sank. He'd been wrong to trust in Hericore's wisdom, and accepted Langdon for what he was – the enemy.

"I'm not comfortable telling you a damn thing, *pal*," Philip said, alerting Rick to the danger.

But before the issue could be pressed, the absconded knight deployed a long awaited plan; one constructed long before they crossed paths.

Langdon elegantly danced to his feet and put Rick to the sword, emptying the detectives belly of its contents. Without any substance to hold him upright, Rick slumped down and left Philip to face the traitor alone.

"I'm sorry, detective. But you shouldn't have been such a good artist," Langdon sadly explained. "You only have yourself to blame, really."

Philip dived for the desk and the revolver within. He was agile, but never wise; the draw was locked. Wasting no time, Langdon used his ballet of war to pin Philip down, holding him with a loud conviction.

"I knew it," he hissed, with quickened breaths.

Langdon's heavy gauntlet came down on his face. A crack was the last thing he heard for a while – a crack, and pitch so high that it numbed every sense.

***

When Philip awoke, night had arrived over the town, and the office was deserted. A pain in his skull removed colour from his vision, and hazed all that surrounded him in a blue mist. Since acquiring time's gift, he'd felt headaches like this before, but never as persistent, slowly torturing his mind and soul.

The stars shone through the gaps in the roof and contrasted against Rick's dark blood, grounding Philip and focusing him on reality. Movement was limited. Even if his muscles weren't so fatigued, Langdon had bound him to a cabinet by a thick line of rope. Wrapped up and forced to share the room with the gloom of death, Philip lost his classic grin and traded it for a gritted set of teeth.

"Hericore, you were wrong," he whispered, "I should have killed the lying piece of… shit!"

For all the moral pride in the world, being the merciful type was the ultimate folly: he was always the person with their back turned, just waiting to be stabbed.

Time passed slowly. The isolation with Rick's vita rapidly drying all around kept his mind locked in the present, unable to venture forward or back. Langdon burst into the office, sweaty and tired.

"Ah, you're awake. Thought my right hook did you in. Seemed like that big brain of yours was leaking out your nose."

"I'd be so lucky. Lest then I'd be spared seeing *you* again."

"Don't be a smart-ass. As I recall you're the idiot that bought my act. A travelling wizard? Really? Did you think I was *that* dumb?" Langdon said. "Anyway, I'm only returning the favour. You kept me alive, so now I'll do the same. If I wasn't so devil-may-care, then I'd represent my boss whole-heartedly and chop you down, right here, right now."

This mysterious 'boss' was aggressively stupid, leaving a task so big to man with a brain so small. If stopping Hericore's plan was so important, then stopping Philip was far from the best way to do it.

"Well then, who do you represent?" Philip asked. "My deeds have attracted countless onlookers as of late," he added, coveting what little reputation he still had left.

"Would you keep it a secret – just between us *pals*?"

Philip recovered his empty grin.

"Never."

The knight was using him for a cheap laugh, but only one jester was allowed in court, and it wasn't him.

"Very cautious people," Langdon answered. "So I hope you'll understand if I keep their names a secret."

"Wouldn't mean anything to me. I haven't walked the fields of Sud in a long time. Since I've left, dozens of civil disputes have consumed the place. I doubt any of the old politicians are left standing."

Langdon laughed. "Who said anything about Sud? Again, I hope you'll understand... In time, perhaps."

Philip understood, but was far from happy with the secrecy. Keeping Langdon talking was the safest plan he had left.

"I'm asking the wrong question," he said, changing his manipulative tactics. "Why?"

"Hericore, your boss, is playing with oblivion's toys. My employers can't have him persist. No one deserves that power."

"Seriously? I took you for a risk-taker."

"I'm taking risks right now," Langdon reminded him. "Even risk-takers need to exercise caution."

Bound, but never boundless, Philip pressed against the knight's patience.

"You're not cautious, you're a coward. Cowering behind an invisible army, living it large on the other side of the planet, all while you lie and cheat us heroes." Langdon ignored his words and grabbed Rick's documents, then started to pile them up in the centre of the room atop the desk, disorderly and with speed. "No evidence? That doesn't bode well for me."

"This isn't about you or your creed. This is for my own allegiance. My family."

"Family?" Philip chuckled. "This is all about that mysterious brother, isn't it?"

"Right you are. He was my partner in crime, back home. Always was a renegade, and now is no different. Seems he found himself caught up with the group Rick was tracing." Langdon showed him the sketch one last time. "When I saw this face, I knew the mission needed to accelerate."

Blood boiled in them both. Neither of them enjoyed this stand-off. The silver knight went quiet, and continued to gather papers.

"Killing Rick and capturing me was foolish; premature, even. You'll regret your actions once Thomas finds me tied up in this mess," he warned.

"Tommy won't be coming. I spiked the beast's drinks. He'll be down and out for a while – long enough for you to work on that tan, and for me to finish up some unfinished business. Besides, he failed to notice me lugging Rick and his accompanying viscera out of town."

Rick was a Greycoat, the best breed of survivor the west had to offer. What did this make Langdon? Whoever held the knight's service was too powerful for a single flag, a single code... they were a union victorious.

"Why kill Rick? You'd spare me, but not him?" Philip asked.

Pacing nervously around the room, peering out into the desert sands, Langdon was worried. Yet his big mouth kept flapping as he grew ever closer to rounding up all of Rick's work before leaving Philip as abruptly as he found him; a meeting that wasn't by chance.

"Rick was a leech stuck to my brother's side, and I was obligated to remove him," Langdon said, but his voice softened. "He was one hell of a fighter. Kept groaning till I ditched him in the sands north of here. The bannasites will enjoy eating his corpse, a meal prepared right here in this room."

"You sound regretful."

"Then that makes two of us." The knight squatted down and took a deep breath of relief, composing his sweating form. "But we shouldn't dwell on it. 'Prepared regrets? Goodbye victory'."

Those words, they meant something to the people of Caster, and to some more than others. Opposing Sud de Baie were the soldiers of Rouge Tarus, a warring power in the Casterlands known for their deep red colour, a symbol of the blood they let. In his moments of weakness, Langdon didn't speak wisdom from Sud, but rather the words of the raging Tarus.

"Mortimer vorde? Bonvo victoria. Words to live by... if you're a red cloak, that is," Philip said, triumphantly calling out the chink in Langdon's vocal armour.

The silver knight jumped in place.

"What! That doesn't mean–"

"It means plenty to me. I'd suggest–"

Philip's advantage was cut short by voices in the distance, chatting from a group of travellers near the shack; voices he recognised. Among them were Helena's sass-filled remarks and Hericore's words of wisdom. His allies had arrived.

"Shit!" Langdon fretted, peering outside. "I thought we had more time."

"I'm always out of time these days. Looks as if it's your time to pay the piper."

The knight paced for a time. As the Drakeguard came closer to the town and the shack, his options declined by the seconds that passed. Even after the betrayal, Philip pushed for a better end to this conflict, determined to salvage what little kindness was left in his relationship with Langdon.

"You could run, Langdon. Run and hide with this strange brother of yours, until my warriors and I have moved on. You've made yourself known and have a few choices left."

"No! I can't, not now. If I return with nothing after coming this close, I dread to think of what punishment my superiors will dish out."

Unlike earlier, the fleeting hope was genuine, and Langdon feared the coming storm. The knight sweated more, and vomited onto the pristine drawing of his brother. It all culminated in an even hastier stacking of Rick's work.

"I guarantee, the wrath my team will show you is far worse. Those who run may face a dishonourable life, but those who fight are doomed to die a dishonourable death," he said. As the papers piled up, it became clear that Langdon didn't want survivors. This devil did care.

When everything was in position, Langdon wiped away his nerves, pulling a block of flint from within the busted drawers of the desk. Fire was always a good way to cleanse one of accountability and mistake. A favoured way to burn both bridge and burden, alike.

"I wish we didn't have to end like this, Phil," the knight panted remorsefully. "If things were different I'd–"

"Save it. No apology is better than an empty one."

With a quivering hand, Langdon sparked the flint on his armour, forcing it to lose its sheen and set Rick's legacy ablaze.

"No more shining armour..." Langdon wallowed, fixed on the dulled plating. "*Bonvo*. May we meet again as equals, Philip."

"Last chance, pal. You shouldn't do this. *It's the wrong move*. You'll die!"

"Maybe. But as you said: 'life is all about the bad decisions.' And who knows, maybe I'll crawl back victorious."

Philip was left alone once more, this time in the burning home. A smokescreen covered the dim knight as he left the fire and headed for the scalding frying pan that awaited him. Rick's blood turned to fine ash at Philip's feet, and the ropes that bound him burned away, freeing the captive hero.

Racing after Langdon, he hoped to stop the knight from paving a trip to Etheriam in the flesh and bone of the Drakeguard. Kindness was lost to Philip, and would be hard to restore. Helping his scaly mentor was a start.

Chapter 18: One Man Army

Harlan and company finally entered Karin. Feeling refreshed and full of vigour, they moved for Declandale.

Days of evading the Order and crossing their lazily-monitored borders had paid off, for some more than others. The journey was a patchwork of begging for free passage in carts or the mercy of a free room, and even the occasional acquisition of some more pyrus. It felt wrong to wheel, deal, and steal, but all this roguery was reminiscent of the old days, before the dwarf's name was the stuff of legend.

In these days they'd even managed to lose Travis for a time, finding the cleric under the arrest of the Order's border patrol. Bella disappeared too, carrying a message to one of their 'friends' down in Yellemette. This plan south was smooth as the coarse flats they trekked through. The ground was harsh, but one thing softened the trip.

Since Lake Vita, Lucille always offered Harlan a smile in place of the same boring stare that everyone else received. The flash flood did more work for the dwarf's charisma than any words could achieve. All that remained now was to make the first solid advance on her and ask the important question.

The question would seal the fates of the two for a long time, and thinking about it summoned a feeling of queasiness within. A difference between love and hate was at stake for them, which put Harlan in an anxious mood also, another foreign concept to welcome.

Lucille led the group along with Haruka, both letting the past stay where it belonged, forging a precedent for all the group's friendships. Haruka's strategic mind kept everyone off the main roads, and instead left them tracking across the dry plains of the savannah, an unstoppable march of determined freedom fighters in the making.

Travis kept close, in front with Harlan and Hericore, who found comfort in conversing about the Great War. It slowly became a favoured topic of the insight-hungry cleric.

There was no doubt in Harlan's mind that Travis wouldn't have lasted a single battle in that war, which challenged the bodies and brains of all who had been stupid enough to partake. He saw leagues of pride-drunk men line up alongside the actual drunken regiments of dwarves as they fended off overwhelming odds, all for what was good and free.

Looking back on those hellish years, Harlan found little good in the violence or freedom, but that was the supposed point: years of war, for centuries of peace.

"Did you ever face death during the war?" asked Travis.

"A silly question to ask. Everyone faced death, every day," the dwarf replied.

"An undoubted truth. But what was your closest call?"

"This curiosity of yours is dangerous," Harlan warned the eager cleric. "But since you asked, it was the battle of Mount Magmaddon that almost ended me. I was outnumbered seven to one against the orcish army, and my men were dropping fast. If the molluskan marines hadn't showed up, well... I and most of dwarfkind, wouldn't be here today."

"You're welcome!" Hemora called from the back of the trail. Hemora was just like his ancestors, and acted as though he'd been personally responsible for turning the tides of war. Harlan let the molluskan have his pride, as he needed it no longer. Who needed pride when you're smitten.

"Fascinating. I was stuck in the east for most of the war, so I never experienced a battle with the orcs. I mostly faced hordes of elven warriors," said Hericore. "They were no push-overs, don't get me wrong. But still, I would love to have relived the war. From a different perspective, clearer truths can be seen."

"Can tell you never sat on the front lines. You'd change that statement quicker than your undies during a real skirmish," Harlan said gruffly. "Smelled of ash, blood, and tears, all while snow and wind burnt at our extremities. Hell of a time."

The drake nodded. "Indeed. But we must return to our warring ways. Once we reach Barsameil, it'll be an all-out war."

Their days spent running from the Order had almost wiped the threat of King Barsalt from all memory. Kings came and went, and Harlan had seen at least a dozen golden kings of Barsameil fall over the centuries. They claimed to be mighty, but were as frail as any other men.

"The Matter Stone – is it the cure for your curse?" Harlan questioned the drake.

"Not alone. My Guard found my name inscribed on an ancient prophecy. 'Once all Primal masters yield to the end, then the curse shall be lifted.' With Time in our palms and Matter being are next goal, our gaze must then seek the other two Stones."

The idea of seeking even more Stones made Harlan's feet and heart ache from exhaustion; saving the world had a steep cost.

"And is whacking the King gonna be a quick job?" he continued to dig.

"We've a mole in his ranks. He's got more than a few reasons to see King Barsalt dead. We'll have a plan, and that's all I know." Hericore sounded more remorseful with each remark. Cold feet were to be expected at some point.

Lucille overheard their chat, and sensed the tension from a fair distance. Stopping to face the drake, she argued her point once again.

"I'm sure we don't need to kill him or anyone else. We could–"

"Everyone shut it!" called Helena, striking the air with a fist of caution.

The whole convoy was soon halted as she demanded everyone's silence and immobility. With finesse, the gunslinger lowered herself to the ground with an ear pressed to the sand.

"What's the hold up?" asked Hemora, stomping his shell foot down. "We're almost–"

"Shhh!" she said, and listened to the ground once more.

It was soon apparent to Harlan what worried her so, as a rumbling could soon be felt shaking beneath them. There was something burrowing below, a common threat one learned to sense after an extensive time in Karin. This was the early warning signal of a bannasite attack.

The wretched worms loved to prey on fresh meat, striking fear into all novices to Karin, seasoned travellers and first-timers alike. Only he and Helena understood the origin of the vibrations, and didn't hesitate to pass an explanation to the others.

"Bannasites!" Harlan shouted, alerting the more educated members of the group, but dumbfounding the rest.

"Banna- what?" Hemora gawked.

"We need to reach Declandale. I don't intend to have my face burnt off by some chunky parasite," Helena complained. But Lucille stopped them from proceeding further, alerting them to another problem slowly dragging its way forward.

Filling the air with the stench of carrion, a member of the Greycoats pulled his prone body through the sand. Fighting against an open wound, the man was pursued by a silver knight, baptised in soot, with vengeance in his eyes. The knight approached them without slowing, and held a valiant look of duty while doing so.

"We need to help him," Lucille begged.

"Where have I heard this before?" Helena asked. "If we make any sudden movements, the bannasites will tear us apart."

The man was almost dead, and smelled as much. Lucille meant well, but prolonging the end would be far from mercifully. Eventually, the Greycoat was stopped by the knight less than twenty feet from the team.

"Stubborn isn't compliment enough for you, Ricky," the knight said to the dying man. "Now be a good hound. *Play dead!*"

"Langdon... I," said Rick, pain numbing his speech. "I... Can't–"

"Then allow me to do the honourable thing and assist."

Whatever story stood behind these two, intervening would be a death-wish. But Lucille, ever the kind soul, fired an arrow at the knight's feet; the only warning he'd receive.

"Don't you dare!"

"Those who dare pay the devil's due," Langdon replied. "I'll make sure to pay my debts in your blood, Lucille."

"You know my name?"

"I know all of you. It's my job, and has been for some time now."

"You're a Knight of Caster," observed Travis. "What's your place in this mess?"

The silver men of the east were too busy with their own growth to stunt other peoples; Hericore's mission must've been the exception.

"No use in talking. This walking cast has already made plans for us. We're dead meat to him," Rangar said.

"All too right," Langdon applauded, smacking together his silver gloves. Leaving Rick to suffer, the knight dashed at the Drakeguard. The bannasites felt the hulking boots smack the soft sand and joined in.

The sluggish creatures burst forth from the ground, their gluttonous bodies bringing up tall geysers of sand. One sent Harlan flying, launching him yards from the carnage.

Kenneth caught him before they slammed head-first into a boulder, covering both of them from head to toe in a thin coating of Karin's iconic, sunburned sand.

"Nice catch," he thanked the old man.

"Don't mention it. I was bound to do something right, one day."

Many more blasts of sand shot from the earth as a dozen bannasites jumped into the air like acidic, overweight dolphins; slowly, they swarmed the group.

Meanwhile, Haruka was combating Langdon in a match of speed and reflexes. Harlan lost more than little time watching the wisps of red and silver spin around each other, resembling a work of art more than a duel. They danced well, keeping a professional edge to their steps and flips. When her shoto clashed with the knight's sword, the clang was quick and high-pitched. Soon, their dance was accompanied by a choir of clangs: like a song played on a dozen tea-bells.

"Protect Hericore. Protect your commander!" ordered Helena, as she and

Travis formed an inadequate phalanx around the drake.

A lone bannasite overshot its attack on Harlan, vaulting over his bald head, and landing instead on Kenneth's arm; screams of agony ensued for the poor fisherman. Bannasites used a potent acid to open up a victim's flesh, only to poison the blood below, eventually killing them; but not after sending them to a bitter coma first.

While Kenneth struggled, Harlan did manage to get a clear look at the foul worm – something he'd never achieved in his long life.

It had the bloated shape of a maggot, but was similar to a leech in colour and features, possessing a sucker on one end of its body and a stinger on the other, strikingly akin to a wasp's. The sucker had triangular, jagged rows of teeth lining it, a useful tool for burrowing deep. The stinger was being thrust at Kenneth's face, attempting to gouge at his eye sockets, while the creature's slimy body remained coiled around the arm.

Still emptying his lungs with agonising screams, Kenneth fell to his knees.

"It burns. It burns!" he shrieked. The chemical smell overpowered the burnt flesh. "Help me, Harlan. Help me, you sonofabitch!"

"Blimey, what in all the holy gospels is happening to 'im?" Travis blurted out, losing his posh veneer once more.

"I believe... *it's dissolving his flesh,*" Rangar faintly commented, going green in the face.

"Great, bet you're glad you've got those scales," Helena said with envy, before lassoing the bannasite away with her whip. Cleansing the maggot in fire, Harlan stepped in to burn the separated parasite to a thin, black crisp.

"Glad to see that thing burn," Kenneth panted. "Cheers."

"Just returning the favour."

They went on to kill another pair of worms. Along with Helena's crack-shots, the mess was starting to clean up. Over the clangs of the Knight, the thunderous cracks of Helena's whip could be heard, adding to the choir – along with Rangar's loud dry heaves, they turned it into an orchestra.

Langdon was still a problem, holding his own against Haruka, Hemora, and Lucille at once. Kenneth attempted to help, but was pushed aside by the knight, not even worth the end of his sword.

"Keep up, old man," Haruka taunted, sounding frustrated in herself.

Fortune favoured Langdon, but it had a costly pay-off: his armour was melting under the bannasite's chemical rain, welding it to the boy's smooth skin.

Atop this, Haruka swiftly landed a poisonous stab to his shoulder. Langdon's fate was sealed, and all subsequence swings were made knowing they'd be his last.

"You think a little pain can kill me? No pain, no gain, little girl!" Langdon cried out, as his onslaught persisted.

More bannasites flooded in, now diving around Lucille, who huddled over Rick, helping to close the gaping wound he bore. Her kindness would be her undoing if Harlan didn't make his next choice. He couldn't let her burn – not like everyone else in his life.

The dwarf dived in between her and the deadly monsters, and it didn't take long until they had wrapped around his own, tender flesh. Luckily, his girth made it impossible for them to make a second loop around his body, reducing his torture – but it was still torture, none-the-less.

The toxic slime touched his suit and clothing and got to work instantly, eating through his prison shirt and scalding the brown skin underneath. It was a cold burn, like ice was pressed against him for an eternity – a worthy punishment for his noble chivalry. It was too much to bear, and his knees faltered. The dwarf slumped to the ground, crying for sweet release.

Lucille moved from Rick and gazed upon Harlan's sacrifice. Raising her bow, she removed each worm with a single volley of arrows. Using his last iota of power, Harlan blasted the wounded creatures to hell, two gruesome infernos burning each other out.

"Harlan, I..." Lucille stuttered, now standing over his ravaged body.

"Go," he whimpered. "They need you more than I."

"That's not true. You've always needed me, you stupid man," she said quietly.

Reaching out, she grabbed his unburned hand and smiled. The soft touch he left could be the last. If so, it'd be an honourable one. He had so many things to say in such a short amount of time – how he felt, and what he wanted for her. But more pressing matters were afoot.

"I said: *go!*" he commanded, sending away his sweetheart.

With no other options than to lay down and watch life pass him by, he witnessed everyone's struggle, a scene he could see with subjectivity for a change.

"Hericore's safety is paramount!" shouted Helena, whipping a pair of parasites from her boss's back. The maggot crawled towards Kenneth, looking to sear another arm. Ready to claim his first kill, Kenneth leaped at the worm, only to have his moment stolen.

Haruka swooped in at the last second, burying her shoto deep in the beast's guts, and claimed it for herself.

"Too slow," she taunted, dissecting it right in front of the fisherman.

Harlan gazed over at Langdon, whose will to survive had pushed him to a great extreme. Rangar and Hemora were both down at his feet, and Lucille's arrows were irrelevant to the knight, bouncing off his armour with an oddly satisfying ping.

Using his trident as a cane, Hemora returned to his feet.

"That all you've got? You dick!" chanted the molluskan, a glutton for punishment.

His call was reinforced by Gerald's supportive whinnies. The horse found comfort watching them battle while he spectated from far. This drew the knight's attention and he gave Gerald a look akin to that of a brother.

"My horse? You stole my fucking horse!" yelled Langdon, kicking away the trident. Hemora fell down a second time, the difference being he didn't arise for a third round.

Haruka was next to drop to Langdon's skill, striking a similar pose to the one she'd been in when Harlan had first met her after the breakout. Kenneth keeled over along with her, the bannasite poison finally dropping him into an eerie sleep.

"That's right, old man. Know your place." Langdon, smirking and shivering, moved past the fallen, towards Hericore.

"No more, Helena," the drake ordered. "No more shall fall for me."

Harlan spotted a look on Hericore's face, one of atrocity and defeat, differing from the faces the drake had pulled prior to this fight. Their fountain of hope had dried up in Langdon's wake.

"With all due respect, boss, screw that. I'm taking this fancy dinner plate down," Helena defied.

Langdon threw down his crumpled shield and charged onwards; the final stand that would define him. With two heart-stopping clicks of two empty guns, Helena's expression turned sour, her devastation escaped in a single word. "Fuck."

Harlan half expected Langdon to cleave her in half from breast to hips. But a single flicker of faith stood up for her – an unlikely act of defiance that she was glad to see. Travis stepped directly in Langdon's path, using a prayer to deflect the lethal blow, throwing the knight off balance.

"'In the name of the Goddess, I, a humble servant of vitality, banish you to Tarus, foul fiend'," said the cleric proudly, with a thick brushstroke of feebleness overriding his noble stance. "May light b... May light banish you!"

Stumbling back on two feet, Langdon mocked this feat of feigned bravery. Not flicker of the Goddess' golden light came to their aid, and Travis hung his head in shame.

"What the hell do you call this? A dress-wearing cleric who wants to get fucked by something other than his cowardice, maybe?"

Raising his head, the cleric smiled, accepting his fate. Without the Goddess or his friends to back him, Travis charged forth.

"No, lad, I call it divine intervention."

Helena fumbled with her gun, jamming a handful of bullets inside while Travis tackled their opponent in a less than optimal way. Playing hero could only work so well, as Harlan had recently found out. Travis was next to discover this cardinal rule.

A slough of punches and kicks were soon halted by Langdon's blade as the knight grabbed a leg and sliced clean through the appendage. Falling past his severed right leg, Travis hit the ground in the fevered sweats of anguish.

Travis joined the rest of the Guard in defeat, crying out over his loss.

Helena wasted no time, refilled Mercy, and gunned down Langdon in fit of rage. Finally, the silver knight gave up with a glad smile on his face.

It was over. Hericore had survived unscathed, but at a huge cost. Everyone else lay beaten and bruised by the single feat of a sooty stranger. The Casterlands made their men tough, that was for certain.

Gerald slowly approached the scene, focusing on his old master, who showed great sorrow to the horse. Losing all aggression, only a drained pool of determination lingered inside of Langdon.

"Ah, Gerald, my dear friend." In one last plea for comfort, he patted the horse's nose. "Don't be afraid. I'm finished, but you… heh heh… must go on."

Philip showed up moments later, covered with the same soot-ridden appearance. Langdon looked up at the boy and exchanged some final words.

"You weren't wrong, Phil," he calmly rasped. "I've failed those who I loved. Honourable, I am not."

"Welcome aboard," replied Philip, hate in his every word. "Bonvo, Langdon."

Harlan found it difficult to keep his eyes open anymore. Additionally, his heart was slowing, and failing to pump his thickened blood through its already narrow veins – it felt like the end. He didn't mind dying for a pretty girl. In fact, it was probably the only way he'd end up.

"Five hundred years of fighting, and I go down to a worm. Heh, bloody brilliant."

But Harlan pushed forward, beating back fate with every last morsel of life he had left. Fortunately for him, as fortune's favour abandoned Langdon, it passed on to a more deserving chump.

Epilogue

Hericore watched as the Guard lay in fragmented ruin upon the sands of Karin, and he oversaw the dismay with a heavy heart. If losing his home wasn't bad enough, now he was without his people and their allegiance.

Helena was the only one still able to stand and along with Philip managed to seek help within Declandale, for a price of course. The kindness of strangers was measured only by a man's wealth these days. Hericore thought of eras past, he lived in the fifth long before its fall and life was so simple back then. Freshly baked bread was free to sit on a man's windowsill without fear of a thief's sticky fingers, children played in the open without being the apple of a creeper's eye, and the Order… The Order was a sign of love and peace, free of the fear and taint that gripped it in recent years.

After the ex-prisoners were carried away on stretchers, Helena helped drag Travis through the sands. Philip was feigning a calm demeanour as he walked his drake's sore hide to the town. The dandy wanted to be something more – something like him – and there Hericore was: the only soldier left unscathed after the battle. What example was he setting for Philip?

Back during the Great War the drake would take a flurry of stabs, jabs, cracks and snaps for his men – it was a commander's duty. But now, he'd be lying if the thought of flying away didn't cross his mind. Whether it was to preserve his own neck or that of the world at large, Hericore wanted to run and run far.

The rest of the night was a mesh of Philip's complaints and criticisms, while Helena helped the healers of the Declandale in their own duty.

Hericore didn't focus on the pain or anger, only his own ill feelings. It was a year ago that he'd set his plans in motion and had organised these plans for a much longer time, but for the first time in a long time he'd actually harboured doubt.

A quick retreat to his tent was a met with a final bout of insults from Philip's upset mouth, but again the words bounced off the drake's thick hide. If Hericore was holding doubts, then sleep would not come lightly. So began a night of reflection in a near hopeless battle to retain some control over the mess Langdon left in his wake. But doubt was an unmoving beast, and Hericore faced two options: live with the monster or run in the face of it. The choice that rung in his mind all night was unfortunately the latter.

<u>Special Thanks</u>

This project wouldn't have been possible without the backing, work, and support of some amazing individuals. These special people are:

Allistair 'AJ' Martin

Brent Skinner

Connor Robinson

Danny Goldsmith

Dom Buchanan

Eleanor Joyce

Genine

Henry Double

Holden Stenner

James Hart

Maureen Robinson

Megan Risley

Michael Grover

Nathan Lee

Pat Barker

Steph Sayer

'The Twins' Tracy and Wendy

Tristan Sayers

Appendix

The Drakeguard Knights:

–Hericore, Arch-Paladin, head of the Order's High Council

–Philip, former Vagabond, Hericore's ward

–Zarpadon, the fallen angel and Hericore's personal assistant

–Helena Starr, former Vagabond, captain of Hericore's Guard

 Bella Starr, Helena's pet bird.

–Ashley 'Ash' Belwert, member of the Guard

–Travis Farland, former Vagabond, Hericore's cleric and doctor

–Thomas Tel-Moot, former Vagabond, member of the Guard

– James Stone, former Vagabond, member of the Guard

–Krell, member of the Guard?

–Gerald, horse of the Guard

–Bella, bird belonging to Helena

The Escapee Prisoners:

–Kenneth Porter, former Central Block prisoner and fisherman with a limited skill set

–Lucille Woodward, former East Block prisoner and hunter, sought for her survival skills

–Harlan Ainsworth, former West Block prisoner and legend, sought for his array of knowledge

–Hemora Vangesh, former West Block prisoner and nobleman, sough for his combat abilities

–Haruka Katowa, former East Block prisoner and assassin, sought for her deceptive talents

–Randell 'Rangar' Garwood-Edwards, former West Block prisoner and mercenary, sought for his combat abilities

–Donsis Allisteel, former West Block prisoner and loan shark, sought for his wealth

Members of the Order:

–Royland, Father, founder of the Order

–Mabel Dirk, Head Banker of the High Council

–Clara Cristel, Cardinal of the High Council

–Ryon Wellington, Battlemaster of the High Council

–Matthias Gilligan, Saint of the High Council

–Percival Hart, Warden of Refracted Light

–Boyd Loyce, Captain of Refracted Light

–Jelz Reltus, Captain of Refracted Light

–Lud Kavel, Paladin under Hart's command

–Hunter, head hunter for the Order

–Daniels, Paladin under Hunter's command

Other Characters:

–Xander Greenhill, former Lord of the Green Isles

–Kalsec, the Moonsabre, mysterious stranger

–Mary, servant of Theoline

–Boris, patron at Trawlers Inn

–Catherine, member of the Wild Cats

–Katherine, member of the Wild Cats

–Gaffer, leader of the Wild Cats

–Opyus, leader of Vipsa

–Bol, member of Vipsa

–Langdon, travelling knight

–Patrick 'Ricky' Morello, Greycoat detective

–Madame Osiris, leader of the Cult of Undying

–Natalia, granddaughter to Osiris

–Dallas, patchwork soldier working under Natalia

–The Beast, patchwork soldier working under Natalia

Gods of Prime:

–Gideon, Great Lord, God of Power, leader of the Primals

–Theoline the Wise, God of Knowledge, Valentine's brother

–Valentine, Mother, Goddess of Love, Gideon's wife

–Bethany the Blessed, Goddess of Life, daughter of Gideon and Valentine

–Lilith, The Reaper, Goddess of Death, daughter of Gideon and Valentine

–Aldrich the Forsaken, God of Undeath, son of Gideon and Valentine

–Aldon, God of the Arcane, creator of elves, banished

–Solaris, God of the Sun, banished

–Luna, Goddess of the Moon, sister to Solaris

–Hugo, Patriarch of Man, God of Jealousy and Fear, creator of mankind

Locations:

–Magnus, land of mortals

–Midgartt, central continent of Magnus

–Vitalands, land of the Order, located in west Midgartt

–Valordolt, capital of the Vitalands

–Bridgeport, city in the Vitalands

–Betiel, city in the Vitalands

–Ryford, city in the Vitalands

–Convict's Cove, town in the Vitalands

–Lumber's End, town in the Vitalands

–Roy's Fork, Village in the Vitalands

–Igial's Lane, Hamlet in the Vitalands

–Casterlands, land of the Caster Council, located in east Midgartt

–Karin Freelands, land of the lawless, located in south-west Midgartt

–Declandale, frontier town in the Freelands

–East Karin, land of the desert dwarves, located in south-east Midgartt

–Barsameil, land of the Barsalt Dynasty, located in far south Midgartt

–Arcwoods, land of the Birch Dynasty, located in north Midgartt

–Ivory Helm, land of the Helm Lordship, located in far north Midgartt–Eastock, the eastern continent of Magnus

–Wasternlands, the western continent of Magnus

–Tealka, the underwater continent of Magnus, under the ocean between Midgartt and Eastock

–Prime, land of the gods

–Etheriam, the waters of heaven

–Tarus, the pits of hell

Items of Importance:

–Time Stone, Tempus Porta, able to manipulate the flow of time, currently in the Drakeguard's possession

–Space Stone, Raumtür, able to manipulate the fabric of reality, whereabouts unknown

–Mind Stone, Mentir Mania, able to manipulate another's perception, whereabouts unknown

–Matter Stone, Yugo Materia, able to transmute any material into another, currently in King Barsalt's possession

–Pyrus, an elemental crystal of condensed heat energy, used by Harlan

–Arcus, an elemental crystal of condensed arcane energy, the material crystivines are made from

–Rouge Candle, a magical remote detonator for arcos runes, build by Bart the Bold, currently in Hart's possession

–Arcos Rune, a magically powered clay explosive

–Rouge Candle, magically-powered remote detonator used by Bart the Bold

<u>Also By Jack Robinson</u>

The Tales of Magnus and Prime: Stone Soul

The Tales of Magnus and Prime: Meeting of the Minds Volume 1

The Prequels of Magnus and Prime: Kadian

Smile

Room 3B-1

To Tell Tall Tales

Available online now. Check us out at:

facebook.com

twitter.com

youtube.com

amazon.com

and

magnusandprime.com

for more.